SOMETHING ROYAL

Other books by Maggie Dana

Kate and Holly: The Beginning (Timber Ridge Riders)
Keeping Secrets, Timber Ridge Riders (Book 1)
Racing into Trouble, Timber Ridge Riders (Book 2)
Riding for the Stars, Timber Ridge Riders (Book 3)
Wish Upon a Horse, Timber Ridge Riders (Book 4)
Chasing Dreams, Timber Ridge Riders (Book 5)
Almost Perfect, Timber Ridge Riders (Book 6)
Taking Chances, Timber Ridge Riders (Book 7)
After the Storm, Timber Ridge Riders (Book 8)
Double Feature, Timber Ridge Riders (Book 9)
Flying Changes, Timber Ridge Riders (Book 10)
Horse Camp, Timber Ridge Riders (Book 11)
Something Royal, Timber Ridge Riders (Book 12)
High Stakes, Timber Ridge Riders (Book 13)

Turning on a Dime ~ a time travel adventure
The Golden Horse of Willow Farm, Weekly Reader Books
Remember the Moonlight, Weekly Reader Books
Best Friends series, Troll Books/Scholastic

Sign up for our mailing list and be among the first to know when the next Timber Ridge Riders book will be out.
Send your email address to:
timberridgeriders@gmail.com

For more information about the series, visit:
www.timberridgeriders.com
Note: all email addresses are kept strictly confidential.

TIMBER RIDGE RIDERS

Book 12

SOMETHING ROYAL

Maggie Dana

PAGEWORKS PRESS

This is a work of fiction. While references may be made to actual places or events, all names, characters, incidents, and locations are from the author's imagination and do not resemble any actual living or dead persons, businesses, or events.
Any similarity is coincidental.

ISBN 978-0-9909498-3-1

Published by Pageworks Press
Text set in Sabon

for Pete

1

"DON'T LOOK," said Kate McGregor, "but I think we're being followed." She propelled her sister into the nearest shop doorway and peered around the corner like an amateur sleuth from one of their aunt's novels. "That girl, over there."

Shading her eyes, Holly Chapman squinted across the village's narrow main street. All she saw were summer visitors meandering along the sidewalk, two boys on skateboards weaving through traffic, and a farmer hauling sacks of grain from the feed store. Nothing suspicious.

"Where?" she said.

Kate sighed. "I guess she's gone."

"You're imagining things again," Holly said.

Last Sunday, they'd been at the Sugar Shack, celebrating the end of horse camp with ice cream sundaes, and

Kate was convinced that a girl at the counter had been watching Holly. But when Holly looked, the girl had vanished. There'd been a couple of kids perched on bar stools, inhaling milkshakes as if their lives depended on it, but no sign of a skinny girl with glittery, two-inch nails and bottle blond hair.

That was how Kate had described her.

But Kate wasn't exactly an expert on hairdos and makeup. When it came to anything more complicated than a ponytail, she could barely fix her own hair—let alone put on mascara without splattering it all over her face—and always asked Holly to do it for her. Yet now, here she was, convinced that the very same girl was following them in Winfield.

Like in broad daylight?

Holly shook her head. She couldn't think of anyone who'd be interested enough in her to become a stalker—not even on the barn's Facebook page. And she'd run into a few whackos there, like the guy who claimed to have been a famous racehorse in a previous life.

Mom had promptly blocked him.

Even so, a worm of unease twisted inside her. Until a year ago she'd been stuck in a wheelchair and was active in chat rooms for disabled kids. She'd made cyber friends all over the world—and they were totally great, except for the girl she'd actually met who turned out to be very different in real life.

Despite the heat, Holly gave a little shudder. She wiped a strand of blond hair off her sweaty face. It had to be ninety degrees out here on the sidewalk. "C'mon," she said, grabbing her bike. "Let's go home. I want to ride Magician."

"And swim?" Kate said.

"You bet," Holly said. "We'll go to the lake."

As they pedaled up the hill, Timber Ridge Mountain towered above them. Ski trails spilled from its peak like dribbles of green paint; a bright yellow cable car snaked its way to the summit, taking hordes of tourists to admire the magnificent views. Down below, in the valley, was the barn.

A lump got stuck in Holly's throat. It always did whenever she saw that old red barn with its rusty weathervane and those lush fields filled with horses and ponies where she'd spent most of her life. Her mom ran the barn and its riding program, and three weeks ago she'd married Kate's dad.

Holly and Kate were now sisters.

Not *step*sisters. They'd both agreed on that. To anyone who asked, they were just plain old sisters, even if they didn't share the same last name and looked nothing alike. Kate had mossy green eyes and brown hair; Holly was blond and blue-eyed.

Her cell phone chirped.

It was probably Adam, her boyfriend, and they'd already texted a dozen times that day. Slowing down as she reached the barn's parking lot, Holly pulled out her phone and checked caller ID. An out-of-area call.

Okay, best to ignore it.

But the phone kept cutting out and then chirping again as if someone was absolutely determined to get hold of her and wouldn't quit until she answered.

"Hello?" Holly said.

Twiggy's voice was so clear that it was hard to believe she was three thousand miles away in England. "I'm coming over," she squealed. "Next week."

"Oh, my god. Really?"

"Yes, really," said Princess Isabel of Lunaberg. "Can you believe it?"

Holly's front wheel hit a rut and she almost fell off her bike. She rarely thought of Twiggy as a princess. But that's what she was, even if her tiny country had been wiped off Europe's map a hundred years ago. Twiggy had explained it all, but Holly couldn't remember. Right now, she didn't even care.

The big thing was . . .

Twiggy was coming to Timber Ridge.

They'd plotted and planned for this but never thought it would happen because Twiggy's father, the fabulously wealthy Prince Ferdinand, refused to let Twiggy out of his sight unless her bodyguard was right behind her.

"Is Stephan coming, too?" Holly said.

"No." Twiggy gave a derisive snort. "My father's hired a security firm in New York, but I'll soon give them the slip."

Holly had no doubt that she would. When they'd been together in London the previous month, Twiggy had duped her hapless bodyguard into believing they would be spending the night at her cousin's house around the corner. In reality, they'd gone to the *Moonlight* premiere, where Adam's old school friend Nathan Crane had swept Twiggy off her feet. The premiere party was fabulous fun—everyone was having a great time—until Twiggy had gotten herself and Adam abducted by pirates.

Well, not exactly pirates, but one of them had tattoos and a huge, bushy beard. They were so inept that Adam had called them the "Three Stooges."

"How's Diamond?" Holly said.

That was Twiggy's horse. She absolutely adored him.

"Fit as a fiddle," Twiggy said. "But I'm worried about Buccaneer."

"Why?" Holly glanced at Kate, parking her bike neatly in the rack that nobody else, except her, bothered to use. Buccaneer was Kate's favorite horse in the whole world, right after Tapestry and Magician. He lived at Beaumont Park in England where Kate and Holly had been just a month ago and where Twiggy was now taking riding lessons.

"He's moping," Twiggy said. "I think he misses Kate."

"Or her Life Savers," Holly said.

Twiggy laughed. "Yeah, those, too."

Holly listened for a few more minutes, then promised to text Twiggy later. With a big smile, she flung her bike against the fence and raced for the barn, barely able to contain her excitement. This was too cool for words—like over-the-top cool with a cherry on top.

"You won't believe it," she said breathing hard.

Kate opened the side door. "Try me."

"Twiggy's coming over."

"Oh." Kate's voice sounded flat. "Here?"

"Of course, *here*, you idiot. Where else would she go?"

"I dunno." Kate shrugged and stepped into the barn, leaving Holly with an irresistible urge to shake her.

C'mon, Kate. It'll be fun!

That was the trouble with Kate. She never got really excited and danced about like a maniac the way Holly always did. Holly hated to admit this about her new sister, but most of the time when cool stuff happened, Kate acted about as thrilled as a flattened pizza box.

As far as Holly knew, Kate had never even said *Squee!* Well, except when she cleared a really big jump on the cross-country course.

* * *

For some reason, Holly's excitement over Twiggy rubbed Kate the wrong way. She liked Twiggy, she really did, but the princess sucked all the air out of a room. No matter who was in it—rock stars, famous actors, or even royalty—Twiggy loomed larger and noisier than anyone else. She smiled, she flirted, she cracked the craziest jokes. And whenever there was an adventure to be had, she was first in line.

"Sign me up."

Nothing fazed her. She'd even joked about being kidnapped which had to have been the scariest thing ever, never mind that the pirates—or whatever they were—had nabbed the wrong kids.

But then Kate remembered. Twiggy *was* afraid of something—Gemini, the difficult horse she'd arrived at Beaumont Park with—and Kate had figured out why.

Gemini had been abused by his trainer.

It wasn't until Kate and Holly had persuaded Prince Ferdinand to sell Gemini and buy back Diamond, Twiggy's old horse, that Twiggy had felt brave enough to get in the saddle again. But Diamond wouldn't be coming to the States with Twiggy, so who would she ride at Timber Ridge?

How about Rebel?

His owner, Jennifer West, was still at Beaumont Park and wouldn't be back until the end of August. Kate had been exercising Jen's horse and knew that the spirited gelding could be a challenge. Rebel spooked at stupid stuff, but all horses did. An old joke that ran around the barn every summer was:

Horses are afraid of only two things: things that move and things that don't.

Smiling to herself, Kate stopped to pat Plug's cute little face and feed Daisy a carrot. Marmalade complained, so she fed him a carrot, too. The rest she saved for Tapestry.

A welcoming whicker rumbled down Tapestry's nose, the way it always did whenever Kate appeared. For a moment, she just stood there wondering how on earth she'd gotten lucky enough to own such a fabulous horse. A shaft of sunlight dappled Tapestry's golden rump; her flaxen mane glistened like the luxurious hair of a Disney princess.

Oh, right. The princess.

Shoving thoughts of Twiggy to one side, Kate slid open Tapestry's door. The horses were in the barn because it was wicked hot outside and the flies were horrendous. Kate wiped a couple off Tapestry's velvety nose, then spoiled her rotten with carrots. In the next stall, Holly was doing the same with Magician.

He leaned across the low partition that separated both horses. Tapestry nuzzled his mane and slobbered carrot juice all over his shiny black neck.

Holly complained. "Hey, I just brushed him."

"Did not," Kate said, laughing.

That broke the ice, or whatever it was that always surfaced whenever Holly talked about Twiggy. Maybe she wouldn't come over.

Kate was of two minds: Half of her loved the idea of having Twiggy around; the other half dreaded it because something was sure to go wrong. Trouble followed Twiggy about like toilet paper stuck to your shoe.

* * *

Holly tightened Magician's girth. Now that horse camp was over, they were free to ride wherever and whenever they wanted, unless, of course, Mom was giving lessons to the riding team.

Like right now.

Magician grunted. Holly told him to be a big boy and suck it up. In her excitement over Twiggy's phone call, Holly had forgotten all about the lesson until now. She'd much rather have ridden to the lake with Kate and taken the horses swimming.

But lessons with Mom were mandatory even if it was much too hot in the indoor arena to be working on half halts, diagonals, and the correct two-point position. A big show was coming up and, as usual, Mom was sweating it.

Mrs. Dean, who ran the Homeowners' Association, demanded blue ribbons and trophies to display at the clubhouse. It was all part of her marketing scheme to get wealthy families to buy overpriced houses at Timber Ridge, and if Mom didn't produce a winning team, she could be out of a job. So could the tennis pro and the woman who coached the club's swim team. They all had to perform.

Holly tried not to worry.

It wasn't easy. Last month Mrs. Dean had fired Mr. Piretti, who'd run the ski area ever since Holly could remember. His daughter, Sue, had been on the riding team, and her brother, Brad, was a local snowboarding star. But, in less than two weeks, the Piretti family had been erased from Timber Ridge—like swiping a whiteboard or hitting the delete key—and now hardly anyone ever spoke of them.

Out of sight, out of mind?

2

If Liz called for one more gymnastic, Kate wasn't sure she could handle it. Her shoulders ached, her thighs burned. Even her eyelashes hurt. At any minute, she would collapse and tumble off her horse in a messy heap.

Splat . . . all over the tanbark.

They'd been circling Holly's mom for twenty minutes. Heels down, no stirrups. No reins either, half the time. With arms outstretched they'd jumped the line, one after another. It was just her, Holly, Angela Dean, and Kristina James. The other team members were scattered all over the place—Jennifer was still in England, Sue had moved to Colorado, and Robin was out there with her. Nobody knew if she or Jennifer would be back home in time for the Labor Day show.

If not, Liz wouldn't have any reserves.

The four riders now waiting for her next command would be on the team by default, whether or not they deserved to be. It hadn't always been this way. When Kate had first arrived at Timber Ridge last summer, competition for the riding team was fierce, and she'd had to prove herself good enough to be on it.

But things had changed.

Right now, Liz didn't have any choices, and this could end up backfiring if her team didn't score big ribbons at the next show. Kate hated this. Winning blue ribbons wasn't what loving horses was all about. It was taking care of them, making sure they were comfortable and well fed and happy about what they were doing. Kate knew that Holly agreed, but there wasn't anything they could do about it. For now, her mom was stuck with Mrs. Dean.

"Kristina," Liz yelled. "Get your elbows in. This is show jumping, not a ballet lesson."

Angela snickered, then got slammed for being on the wrong diagonal. Even Holly didn't escape her mother's relentless criticism.

"Pull Magician's head up," she said. "He'll trip over his feet at any minute."

And just when Kate thought she'd gotten away without being picked on, Liz said, "Tapestry's not paying attention, and neither are you. If you're planning a nap, please do it somewhere else. There's a nice pile of blankets in the tack room."

On and on it went, until Laura Gardner poked her head around the arena door. "Liz, you've got a phone call."

"Where?" Liz patted her pockets.

"In your office."

"Thank goodness," Holly muttered.

"Who is it?" her mother said.

"Mrs. Dean."

Still patting her pockets, Liz strode across the arena. No doubt she'd lost her cell phone again. It was probably on the kitchen counter beneath a pile of mail or kicked behind a tack trunk. You never knew where you'd find it until it sprang into action, and then Liz would act kind of puzzled as if she'd never heard its ring tone before.

No surprise there.

Holly was always changing it. She said it was just to keep her mother in the twenty-first century. Kate knew what that was like. Her father was a brilliant entomologist. He'd led scientific expeditions to the jungles of Borneo and the Amazon, but he'd only just learned how to use email and was totally baffled by Twitter and Facebook. Holly called them *Luddites*, and Kate had to look it up—*people opposed to new technology.*

But right now, it gave them a break.

With sighs of relief, the girls slowed to a walk. The horses relaxed and dropped their heads. On a loose rein, Tapestry vacuumed up tiny bits of hay from the ground.

"Whew, that was rugged," Kate said.

Kristina patted Cody's neck. Her palomino had worked up quite a sweat. "What's gotten into Liz? She wasn't this tough before."

"Yeah," Angela said. "She's—"

"—working us hard to please *your* mother," Holly snapped.

"Well, ex-*c-u-u-u-se* me," Angela drawled. She jerked Ragtime's reins so hard that her bay warmblood snorted and skittered sideways. Angela barely managed to stay on.

Kate masked her sigh with a cough. She wasn't in the mood to tackle Angela right now. She had enough on her mind, what with Holly's stalker that she refused to worry about and Princess Twiggy's imminent arrival.

Oh, and the horse show.

It wasn't the biggest show of the season, but it supported Mrs. Dean's favorite charity and she expected her team to win. Last year, when Liz fired Vincent King, Angela's evil trainer, Mrs. Dean had forced Angela to switch teams and ride for Larchwood instead. They'd taken second place, right behind Timber Ridge. A week later, Angela had returned to the barn, not the least bit embarrassed by her mother's erratic behavior.

Liz didn't appear to be coming back to the arena, so Kate led Tapestry into the barn, followed by the others. While Kate rubbed her mare down, she glanced across the aisle at Ragtime's stall. Ears pricked, he had his head over the door, eager to frisk anyone who walked by in the hopes of scoring a treat.

But Angela didn't care.

She yanked off his saddle and bridle and didn't even bother to run a brush over his sweaty coat, much less throw a cooler on his back. One of these days, he'd tie up and colic. And if he did, Mrs. Dean would toss him out and buy Angela another horse.

Just like she had with Angela's first pony.

At the Festival of Horses, in a moment of unexpected honesty, Angela had confessed to Kate that she didn't dare connect with a horse because the minute she did, her mother would replace it with a better horse—one that would win the trophies and blue ribbons Mrs. Dean craved.

So Angela had distanced herself. She pretended not to care about whatever horse her mother bought, and Ragtime was the latest in a long line of winners.

Everyone loved him—except Angela.

Slowly, the barn emptied out until it was just Holly and Kate. They dumped their saddles and bridles in the tack room and headed for Liz's office. Kate smelled Mrs. Dean's sickly perfume before she even opened the door.

* * *

"Mom," Holly cried, charging into her mother's office. "Twiggy's coming over." She didn't notice Mrs. Dean sitting beside Mom's messy desk until it was too late.

"The princess?" Mom said.

But that was all it took—just one word—and Mrs. Dean's nose twitched. She could smell celebrities from a mile away. They were potential customers for overpriced houses at Timber Ridge.

"A *princess*?" she said.

Her face softened, and whatever she'd been complaining to Mom about vanished as if someone had hit a switch.

Mrs. Dean worshipped royalty.

When they'd been planning the end-of-camp horse show, Angela's mother had refused to include family pony and the obstacle course until Kate told her that the British royal children always entered these classes. Holly had no idea if they did—and neither did Kate—but it had been enough to convince Mrs. Dean.

Ignoring her, Holly said, "She'll have a bodyguard, but they can stay at our house, right?" It would be a tight squeeze, but Holly didn't care. If she had to sleep on the couch and give her bed to Twiggy, so what?

"Sorry," Mom said. "But no dice. We've got Aunt Bea staying with us, remember?"

"But—" Holly protested.

Mom interrupted. "I'm sure the princess and her bodyguard will be far more comfortable in a hotel."

"No need," said Mrs. Dean, puffing herself up like a peacock. "They can stay with us. We have plenty of room and we'd *love* to have them."

Holly gasped.

This was awful. Beyond awful. It was catastrophic. Angela would glom onto Twiggy like a barnacle and never let go. So would Mrs. Dean.

Mom said, "That's very kind of you."

"No problem," said Mrs. Dean. She stood up and smoothed non-existent wrinkles from her black dress. "Now, I must rush. I have to get ready for our *royal* guests."

Desperately, Holly shot a look at Kate, but her face was blank. She didn't give two hoots about Twiggy. In fact, she'd probably be relieved if Twiggy didn't come over at all.

* * *

Holly spent the next three days in agonies of indecision. Not hers, but Twiggy's. A bazillion texts flew back and forth. First Twiggy was coming and then she wasn't. Her father was having second thoughts. The security firm in New York couldn't find a bodyguard who also knew how to ride. By Friday, Holly didn't know what to think.

"Chill out," Kate said. "She'll come or she won't."

Easy for her to say. If Twiggy's father couldn't hire a competent bodyguard for Twiggy, the whole deal was off. He'd gotten even more protective of Twiggy after she'd been kidnapped, and Holly got that, she really did. But here, in Vermont, where nobody knew she was a princess? Twiggy would be a whole lot safer here than she was in London.

Oh, wait—Angela and her interfering mother.

If they spread the word about Twiggy being a princess, Prince Ferdinand would whisk Twiggy back to England faster than a Derby winner. Faster even than Holly's winning round in Gambler's Choice at last year's Labor Day show, when she'd beaten Adam—and that had been wicked fast.

* * *

"Are you okay?" said Marcia Dean. She led Tapestry into the aisle and clipped her onto the crossties.

"Yeah, I'm fine," Kate said.

"You don't look it."

Kate hated to admit, especially to Angela's former stepsister who'd only just turned eleven, that things weren't exactly all right between her and Holly. But Marcia was a great kid and she'd probably understand. She'd survived being Angela's stepsister and their parents' messy divorce, and she was now living with her dad in

New York while spending summers at the barn with her best friend, Laura Gardner.

Marcia adored Tapestry.

At the end-of-camp show, Marcia's father had shocked Kate to her shoes by offering to buy Tapestry for twenty thousand dollars—twice what she was worth—and all because Kate and Holly had rescued Marcia from a blizzard last November.

Mr. Dean could well afford it, but Kate would never sell Tapestry, no matter if Marcia's father offered her a million dollars.

No, not ever.

On the other hand, she knew that Tapestry, as brilliant as she was, couldn't take her where she wanted to go.

The Olympics.

An equestrian fantasy—something that all riders like her dreamed about. Kate gulped. If she had to give up Tapestry and buy another horse, it would only be a stepping stone to yet another horse and another level until she snagged the attention of a sponsor or the United States Equestrian Federation, provided she worked hard and got better and better. With the right trainer, and—

Marcia brought her back to earth with a bump. "Is the princess really coming over?"

"How do you know about her?"

Last Kate knew, nobody had said a word about Twiggy's visit, not even Holly. She'd kept it quiet for fear of jinxing it—and made her mother and Kate promise to keep quiet as well.

Marcia rolled her eyes. "Get real," she said brushing Tapestry so vigorously she jumped sideways. "*Every*one knows about Twiggy."

Angela.

She'd spilled the beans, of course, she had. No doubt her mother had also blasted it all over Facebook and Twitter, and probably the local paper as well.

The princess is coming to Timber Ridge.

* * *

For two days, Holly argued, begged, and cajoled, but Liz remained firm. *No, there wasn't room for Twiggy and her bodyguard at the house.*

"I'll move back home," Aunt Bea offered. "Then they can have the spare room."

"Don't be silly," Liz said, tapping Aunt Bea's complicated looking sling. It had more straps and buckles than Marmalade's harness. "You can't even cut your own sandwiches, never mind drive a car. And last I saw, you couldn't fasten your bra, either."

"But, *Mom*—" Holly whined.

Kate shot her a look. "Back off."

With a mutinous scowl, Holly pushed past Kate and flounced out of the kitchen. She'd been so frantic about Twiggy's visit that she didn't seem to care about anything else, least of all Aunt Bea's shoulder. She'd injured it shortly before the end-of-camp horse show that she was supposed to have judged. Luckily, Mrs. Dean had found a last-minute substitution—Sam Callahan, a big-name trainer who wrote articles for *The Chronicle of the Horse*.

And that wasn't all. His son was the melt-worthy Luke Callahan, and every horsey girl from here to the moon was madly in love with him—well, almost.

Angela Dean probably hated Luke Callahan's guts. At the end-of-camp horse show, he'd turned on Angela for being insufferably rude about his little sister's horse—in front of all the other camp kids, too.

Holly and Kate had given each other a high five. They'd finally gotten their own back on Angela for wrecking Liz's wedding dress, and they hadn't had to lift a finger to do it, either.

And now Kate was torn.

Hang out with Holly—sisterly commiseration—or stay in the kitchen and help Aunt Bea finish typing her latest detective novel? Able to use only one hand, it was slow going, and Kate had offered to help, even though her keyboarding skills were minimal. Anxiously, she looked at Holly now slumped on the living room couch like a sack of potatoes.

Angry potatoes.

Aunt Bea said, "Don't worry, Kate. I can manage. Besides, I need a little downtime to think about the next scene." She closed her laptop and lumbered awkwardly to her feet. "I'll be in my room for a bit. Maybe I'll even take a nap."

Aunt Bea. Taking a nap?

This was unheard of. Aunt Bea had more zip than all of them put together. Did her shoulder hurt worse than she was willing to admit? Watching her trundle off, Kate added yet another worry to her list.

3

IT FELT ODD, going to the barn by herself and leaving Holly at the house. Kate had asked her to come—had even pleaded with her—but Holly was live-streaming Luke Callahan's latest win on her laptop and had refused to budge.

"He's rockin' it," she'd said.

Kate had wanted to park herself on the couch beside Holly because who wouldn't? Luke Callahan was show jumping's latest teen heartthrob, and Kate idolized him. But that would've meant giving in to Holly's temper tantrum.

No way. Not this time.

Taking care of Aunt Bea and her busted shoulder was a lot more important than having Twiggy and her bodyguard stay at the house. So what if they stayed at Angela's instead?

It wouldn't be the end of the world.

* * *

Tapestry and Magician were in the back paddock, standing nose-to-tail beneath a tree and swishing flies off one another. Kate pulled a carrot from her pocket, shared it with both horses, and then led Tapestry toward the gate.

Of course, Magician followed.

"Sorry, boy," Kate said, maneuvering past him, "but Holly's geeking out over another guy. You'll have to stay here."

Magician whinnied and paced the fence line, kicking up clouds of dust. It hadn't rained in weeks, and the flowers in the barn's window boxes had all wilted, no doubt because Liz had forgotten to water them.

Mrs. Dean would not be happy.

Her home, and the others at Timber Ridge, had irrigation systems to keep everything lush and impossibly green, despite the current drought. All Kate cared about was having enough water for the horses. She checked the paddock's tub. Half full. She would top it up after her ride.

Okay, so where to go?

There were dozens of trails at Timber Ridge, but all of a sudden, none of them appealed. For some inexplicable reason, Kate wanted company.

She didn't want to ride alone.

With Magician still bellowing about being abandoned, Kate took Tapestry into the barn. Marcia Dean had Daisy in the wash stall and was trying to scrub grass stains off her black-and-white legs.

"Good luck," Kate said.

Bubbles of shampoo drifted across the aisle. One landed on Tapestry's nose, and she snorted with surprise.

"Whoops," Marcia said. "Sorry."

"Wanna come for a ride with me?" Kate said.

Marcia wasn't allowed to ride by herself. None of the younger kids were. Just Kate and Holly and the riding team—and the grown-ups, of course—but even then Liz frowned on it. She insisted that everyone should ride with a buddy because cell phones weren't reliable on the mountain and you never knew when you'd get into trouble.

The way Marcia had last fall.

She'd taken off with Angela's horse to prove she could ride just as well as her stepsister and had run into a freak blizzard. If Kate and Holly hadn't found her—half-frozen beneath a jump on the hunt course—who knew what would've happened?

Marcia dropped her brush in a bucket of soapy water. "You mean it?"

"Of course, I do," Kate said, putting her mare on the crossties. "And you can ride Tapestry."

"But who will you ride?"

"Rebel," Kate said.

Jennifer's horse was in his stall, looking terminally bored. He needed a good run. And besides, it was always fun to watch Marcia riding Tapestry. They'd won reserve champion at the horse-camp show, much to Angela's disgust—and her mother's.

After Marcia turned Daisy outside to keep Magician company, she got busy brushing Tapestry, and Kate had to admire the way she did it. Quietly, efficiently. She'd had plenty of practice, taking care of Angela's super-expensive horses, grooming them to perfection and getting no thanks in return.

But not any more.

Angela was now on her own—no more willing Cinderella to do her dirty work—and it showed. Ragtime's coat was dusty, his hooves dull, and his braids always unraveled at shows. Kate was surprised that Mrs. Dean hadn't hired a groom, given Angela didn't even know how to wield a brush or clean her own tack.

Or didn't want to learn.

Marcia didn't need any help with Tapestry, so Kate turned her attention to Rebel. Jennifer's chestnut gelding nudged her pockets, hoping for a treat. His favorite was vanilla pudding, which meant that all the barn kids had spoiled him rotten. So had Kate. Just thinking about it made her teeth twinge.

"You'll get cavities," she warned.

That's what Jennifer always said, but her horse didn't care. Rebel gave a little snort. After inhaling Kate's carrots, he opened his mouth for the bit, then chomped on it noisily while Kate saddled him up. She took him outside and mounted. Marcia was already on Tapestry.

"Where to?" Kate said.

Marcia grinned. "The hunt course?"

"Okay," Kate said. "But no jumping the big ones."

"Spoil sport," Marcia said.

They rode the woodland trail side by side. Marcia had a light touch on Tapestry's reins, unlike her stepsister who always yanked at Ragtime's mouth.

Stepsister?

It reminded Kate of Holly—even though they'd agreed they were sisters, not stepsisters—and Kate couldn't help wondering what Holly was doing right now. Was she missing Kate and wishing she'd come for a ride instead of obsessing over Luke Callahan?

Holly loved the hunt course, and so did Kate. It was her favorite place on the mountain, even better than the cross-country course, where she'd almost lost her job at Timber Ridge last summer.

Breaking all of Liz's rules, Kate had raced Angela over jumps and through water hazards. They'd gone head-to-head at the palisade, and Kate had been about to take the lead when Angela had veered off the trail and jumped a barbed-wire fence.

No way would Kate jump that.

Not even on Buccaneer, and he'd been raring to go. Instead, she'd pulled up and allowed Angela to win their idiotic race.

Buccaneer.

Kate couldn't get him out of her mind. He was like a song that got stuck in your head and refused to let go. Last summer, the willful black horse had arrived at the barn in a total lather. Nobody could get near him—not even Liz—until Kate discovered, quite by accident, that Buccaneer would sell his soul for a handful of peppermint Life Savers. Without thinking, Kate checked her pockets.

No Life Savers.

She didn't need them any more. Buccaneer wasn't coming back to the States. Not ever. He had a good home at Beaumont Park and—

"Are you mad at my father?" Marcia said.

"Why?" Kate said.

"For wanting to buy Tapestry."

"She's not for sale."

"I know," Marcia said. "But Dad told me to ask." She patted Tapestry's golden neck. "You know, just to make sure."

Kate sucked in her breath. She'd known this would come up sooner or later, and now that it had, she didn't know how to handle it.

Last year, when she and Holly had rescued Marcia

from the Halloween blizzard, Henry Dean wanted to reward them. When they'd both refused, he'd switched gears and had insisted on helping Kate's father buy the butterfly museum.

A good investment, he'd said.

This meant that Kate wouldn't have to move out West where her father had been offered another job. They could stay in Vermont. Kate owed a lot to Mr. Dean, but she couldn't bring herself to let him have Tapestry.

"I'm sorry," she said.

"It's okay," Marcia said.

But it wasn't. Kate knew how much Marcia wanted her own horse, and Mr. Dean could afford it, a hundred times over. He could buy Marcia an expensive, prize-winning pony, but all she wanted was Tapestry.

As they rode onto the hunt course, Kate thought long and hard. There were options, and she forced herself to consider them.

If—and it was a very big *if*—she let Marcia have Tapestry, the only way it would work was a lease. That way, Marcia's dad would pay for Tapestry's upkeep—including shoes and vet bills—and Tapestry would stay at the barn. She'd be right there, in her stall or the back paddock, the way she always was, waiting for Kate to spoil her rotten with hugs and kisses and carrots. But how would Kate buy another horse and afford to keep it?

That was the big question.

Kate had no money, and now that Dad had bought the butterfly museum, he didn't have any spare cash either. She'd been over this again and again with Holly, and neither of them had the answer. Rebel shied at a rock.

"Hey," Kate said, pulling her scattered wits together. "Take it easy."

Marcia giggled. "He's a sugar junkie."

After circling the meadow to warm the horses up, they took turns jumping the hunt course, then jumped it side by side. Kate and Rebel took the high fences, while Marcia rode Tapestry over the lower ones. She did an amazing job. Classic, almost. Kate told Marcia to go again.

On her own.

Unlike Angela, Marcia didn't throw herself up her horse's neck as she rode the jumps; her arms weren't bent like a praying mantis. There was a straight line from her elbows, through the reins, to Tapestry's mouth. Her legs stayed where they needed to be.

Kate felt herself relax.

It was absolutely wonderful to be out here, watching Marcia ride Tapestry, until something—she had no idea what—made her glance at the far hedge.

On its other side, Mrs. Dean's bulldozers were eerily silent. Just mounds of orange dirt remained, remnants of her efforts to turn Timber Ridge Mountain into an ugly theme park. Even the younger riders had objected. They didn't want a noisy alpine slide right next to the hunt course with carts clattering down the slope and kids hanging on for dear life and screeching like banshees.

"It'll drive the horses nuts," Laura had wisely said.

Marcia had agreed with her.

So had Vermont, but for different reasons. Mrs. Dean's earth-moving equipment had inadvertently dug up an ancient Native American burial site that was protected by state law, and work on the theme park had come to a halt.

* * *

Holly punched the air with her fist when Luke Callahan scored a blisteringly fast clear round at the Vermont Classic.

"Yes!" she cried.

This put him in first place, ahead of Olympic superstars like Reed Kessler and Will Hunter. At only sixteen, Luke Callahan was already in the adult jumper division. For a second or two, his face filled the screen. He was just as gorgeous on her laptop as he was in real life. Holly sighed. If she wasn't dating Adam, she'd throw herself at Luke—along with a million other girls.

Her cell phone beeped.

Was that Luke? Calling to declare his undying love? After all, he *had* spoken to her at the end-of-camp show. Feeling foolish, Holly checked. No, it wasn't a call or a text message, it was e-mail. But who from? She didn't know anyone called "Misty." The one-liner said:

I.C.U.

Intensive Care Unit? Like in a hospital? That's where Holly had been right after the accident that put her in a wheelchair. Puzzled, she said the letters out loud and felt even more foolish when they sprang into life.

I. See. You.

Misty, whoever she was, had to be one of the kids from Holly's old chat rooms. She didn't dare reply to something like this. It would only reopen old wounds she'd spent the last three years working to heal.

She jabbed the trash can icon.

Misty and her cryptic e-mail disappeared from the phone's memory, but not from Holly's. Maybe it wasn't a bitter kid. Maybe it was—she gulped—that stalker Kate was so worried about.

No, that was stupid.

Impossible. Nobody in their right mind would bother to stalk her. But even so, she wouldn't tell Kate about Misty's e-mail. Kate would only get her knickers in a knot, and Holly could hardly blame her. If it hadn't been for Kate's suspicious mind, they'd never have found Magician when he'd been stolen last summer or rescued Tapestry from being hauled off to slaughter.

Holly's phone pinged again.

Taking a huge breath, she dared herself to look. A text from Twiggy. Was it good news this time?

4

WHEN KATE GOT BACK TO THE BARN, she heard Holly in her mom's office talking to Angela. Snippets of conversation wafted through the half-closed door.

"Twiggy hates broccoli."

"Okay, we won't feed her any."

"And make sure—"

What on earth was going on? Quietly, Kate left Rebel's saddle and bridle in the tack room and crept closer to Liz's office. Moments later, Angela swept through the door, followed by Holly. Neither of them appeared to notice Kate, flattened against the wall and hidden in the shadows.

She felt like a spy.

This was ridiculous. She shouldn't be spying on Holly. They were sisters. They were beyond secrets, weren't they? But Kate wasn't sure any more. Ever since Twiggy announced she might be coming over, Holly had changed.

Like she had in England.

From the moment Twiggy had arrived at Beaumont Park, she'd driven a wedge between Kate and Holly, whether or not she'd meant to. Holly loved horses. She mucked stalls and got thoroughly grubby cleaning tack. But, unlike Kate, she also loved glitz and glamour, and it wasn't long before she'd been pulled into the princess's dazzling world where nail polish outranked hoof dressing, muk shampoo replaced Show Sheen, and braiding elastics weren't nearly as much fun as the sparkling tiaras from Twiggy's overflowing jewelry box.

Kate had been left in the dust.

She'd had no clue how to handle it then; she had even less of a clue now, especially with Angela and her mother involved.

Okay, so what next?

Confront Holly, or pretend she'd never seen them? She could still hear Holly and Angela talking, somewhere out in the parking lot, but their voices were blurred, indistinct. Were they making plans?

Holly and Angela?

Marcia had already left the barn, so Kate slipped into Tapestry's stall. Feeling desperately alone, she wrapped her arms around the mare's warm neck and hung on as if she never wanted to let go.

Like, *never*.

* * *

Dad was having fudge ripple ice cream with Holly when Kate stumbled into the kitchen far later than she'd planned to. Quickly, she pulled herself together and faked a smile.

"Been riding?" Dad said.

"Yeah," Kate said. Her father had blobs of chocolate on his beard. She yanked a paper towel off the roll and handed it to him.

"Thanks," he said, rubbing vigorously.

Kate pointed. "You missed one."

"Where?"

"Your nose."

With a rueful grin, Dad wiped it off. "Holly tells me that her young princess is coming over."

Her princess?

"She's Kate's princess, too," Holly said.

That's a stretch, Kate thought as she helped herself to ice cream from a messy carton on the counter. Twiggy was nobody's princess but her own.

Kate shoved the half-melted ice cream back into the freezer where it would, no doubt, get all covered in frosty bits and end up being tossed out. Slowly, she turned, not sure what to expect.

But Holly was smiling at her, which was far better than the casual indifference Kate had gotten earlier when she'd begged Holly to go trail riding with her. She inhaled a spoonful of ice cream.

Cold pierced her brain like a bullet.

Kate slapped a hand over her mouth. That tooth she'd been ignoring since they got back from England had just reminded her that she needed to see the dentist.

Holly looked up. "What's wrong?"

"Nothing," Kate said. "It's just cold."

"Well, duh-uh," Holly said. "It's ice cream."

Kate probed the sore tooth with her tongue. It was way in the back, but it felt pretty much okay, now that the first shock had worn off. Maybe it was just supersensitive or something. "So, when's Twiggy coming over?"

"Thursday."

Four days.

"Is she staying with Angela?" Kate already knew this. Given what she'd overheard in Liz's office, it sounded as if Holly was jumping ship and joining forces with the enemy. But maybe Kate had misunderstood. Or maybe Liz had changed her mind about them all bunking in together.

She hoped not.

No way did Kate want to share her bedroom with the princess. There was barely enough space for her and Holly, which was why Dad and Liz wanted to buy the house from Mrs. Dean and make it bigger.

Something else to worry about.

The last thing Mrs. Dean wanted was for Kate and her

father to own a house at Timber Ridge, and she'd do everything possible to block the sale, no matter what.

"Yeah, but Twiggy will be with *us* all the time, not Angela," Holly said, finishing off her ice cream. "She'll be here until Labor Day."

This was Kate's biggest fear.

A whole month of Princess Twiggy, her oversized personality, and her new bodyguard. He'd probably be even creepier than Stephan. But Twiggy wouldn't give a toss . . . provided she could outwit him.

* * *

Twiggy's flight was delayed. Bad weather over Boston, according to Angela's latest text. It felt kind of weird to be texting with Angela like this. Holly had known her since kindergarten, and Angela hadn't changed a bit from the bratty kid who always threw a tantrum when she didn't win blue ribbons in her walk-trot classes or get gold stars for her crappy art projects.

This was exactly the same.

Angela wanted first dibs on the princess, so Mrs. Dean had driven her to the airport to meet Twiggy. Much to Holly's surprise, they'd invited her to go, too, but Mom had needed help with new students and she'd put Holly and Kate in charge of the beginners.

It was worse than horse camp.

Amid the chaos of kids and their ponies, Holly kept

checking her phone. Texts from Twiggy—even more from Angela. Finally, they met in the VIP lounge where an attentive British Airways steward handed Twiggy off to the Deans. Angela's mother had captured it all on her cell phone.

Holly glared at the video of Twiggy hugging Angela, then almost choked when another video arrived of Mrs. Dean hugging Twiggy.

Mrs. Dean? Hugging someone?

Jealousy shot through Holly like hot lava. She tried to shake it off, but this should've been her at the airport meeting Twiggy—not Angela and her evil mother.

It was Mom's fault.

For a few moments, Holly steamed. She snapped at her mother, at Kate, and at anyone else who crossed her path, especially these pesky beginner kids. Thanks to them, Angela had already gotten her hooks into Twiggy. By the time they got back to Vermont, Twiggy's fate would be sealed. She'd be trapped inside Angela's gilded tower with no hope of escape. Unless, of course, she let her blond hair down like Rapunzel.

But who'd rescue her?

Adam?

Holly would kill him if he did, never mind that he'd always wanted to be a knight in shining armor. But what about Kate's old boyfriend, Nathan Crane, who'd set a bazillion female hearts on fire in *Moonlight*?

Last Holly heard, they were making a sequel. Maybe Nathan would swing by Timber Ridge on his way to a location shoot in Transylvania, pluck Twiggy from the Deans' impregnable castle, and bring her to the barn atop his black-and-white steed like he had in *Moonlight*, thanks to Adam stunt-doubling for him. That would be totally awesome.

Better than a Disney princess film.

Yeah, right.

Nathan wouldn't know a black-and-white steed from a panda bear, let alone how to ride it. Forcing herself to smile, Holly saddled Plug for an excited seven-year-old and tried to remember what stories about Angela she'd shared with Twiggy when they were at Beaumont Park.

Had she even mentioned Angela?

Probably not, given that she'd been having way too much fun with Twiggy, swapping nail polish and trying on each other's clothes. The sapphire blue cocktail dress Twiggy had loaned her for the *Moonlight* premiere was now in Holly's closet, along with the gold necklace. It had a cluster of diamonds at the center. Holly had been scared to death of losing it.

"It's just a fake," Twiggy had said, shrugging. "You can keep it. I've got dozens more."

Same with the dress.

The princess's walk-in closet held more glamorous gowns, glitzy purses, and designer shoes than a Broadway theater's costume department—none of which Twiggy cared two cents about. When Holly had first met her, Twiggy was wearing frayed denim shorts and scruffy paddock boots with lime green laces. No makeup, either.

"Can I get on now?" said the girl.

With a sigh, Holly nodded. She gave the beginner a leg-up, adjusted her stirrups, and led Plug to the outside arena, where Kate was already coaching two kids riding Snowball and Daisy.

It was going to be a long afternoon.

* * *

While Holly coped with her anxiety by swimming laps in the backyard pool, Kate decamped to their bedroom with her diary. She had her own anxieties to deal with.

She opened to a fresh page and started a list. Things often became less scary when you wrote them down. It took away their importance, reduced them to mere words that were far more manageable than the actual worries were. Trouble was, even now, looking at her scribbled notes, Kate couldn't figure out what worried her the most.

Was it Twiggy's visit or Holly's stalker? The Labor Day horse show? How about Aunt Bea's shoulder? Or was it Dad trying to buy the house from Mrs. Dean?

Kate's back molar twinged. "Ouch."

She added "tooth" to her list.

Was there anything else she needed to worry about? Kate chewed the end of her pencil. Oh, yes.

Marcia and Tapestry.

Reading the list again, Kate's heart sank. She couldn't do anything about *any* of this stuff. It was beyond her control. Well, except for her stupid tooth. She could make an appointment with the dentist. But, too late to call now. It was almost six, and—

The bedroom door banged open.

Holly charged in, dripping water and waving her cell phone. If Kate didn't know better, she could've sworn that smoke was pouring out of Holly's ears. Her eyes blazed, her hands shook. She collapsed onto her bed amid a flurry of stuffed ponies. Furtively, Kate slid her diary beneath a pillow. Nobody knew about it, not even Holly, and they shared almost everything. "What's wrong?"

"As if you don't know."

That much was true. Of course, Kate knew what was wrong. Angela and her mother had taken charge of Twiggy and cut Holly out, completely. From the look on Holly's face, it was obvious Twiggy hadn't gotten in touch since landing in Boston.

"I'm sorry," Kate said.

"Yeah, right." Holly twisted herself toward Kate and her favorite pony fell onto the floor. She scooped it up and hugged it so hard that a lump of stuffing flew out.

“Whoops,” Kate said.

Still hugging the black-and-white pony, Holly said, “I know you don’t like Twiggy. I get that, I really do. But—”

“Not true,” Kate protested.

Holly waved her off. “It’s important to me. Okay? This is a big deal, and Angela’s messing it up.”

Kate added another worry to her list—making sure that Holly didn’t totally freak out over this.

5

HOLLY TOSSED AND TURNED, haunted by dreams of chasing Twiggy along endless corridors but never quite catching up to her. She awoke every half hour and checked for messages. Why hadn't Twiggy gotten in touch? Had Angela confiscated her cell phone? Was the princess a prisoner at Castle Dean, trapped behind a moat of fake waterfalls and giant goldfish?

At five thirty, Holly gave up trying to sleep and hauled herself out of bed. Yawning and bleary eyed, she peeked out the window. It was just getting light; even the birds were still asleep. So was Kate, arms wrapped around Holly's favorite stuffed pony that she'd given her last night.

A peace offering, sort of.

Holly wasn't sure if they'd had an argument, but they'd certainly had something troublesome that needed to be sorted out. First, though, she had to sort out Twiggy.

On her way through the kitchen, Holly grabbed an energy bar and a carrot—then grabbed a couple more and stuffed them into her pockets.

Grass, damp with dew, soaked her sneakers as she ran across the back lawn. Kate's father had mowed it yesterday and clumps of fresh clippings lay strewn about. It would be so tempting to scoop them up for the horses. But all that grass would be a recipe for disaster, like setting toddlers loose in a candy store.

Worst case for the kids?

They'd get a tummy ache and throw up. But horses had a one-way digestive system and couldn't throw up if they ate too much.

Hello, colic.

Munching her energy bar, Holly headed for the barn. In the early morning light it looked almost ethereal. Mist hung over the weathervane and drifted around the paddock, making the horses look as if they were treading on clouds. Magician saw her coming and let out a piercing neigh.

He knew there'd be carrots.

Holly pulled the biggest one from her pocket, fed it to Magician, then gave another to Tapestry. Daisy and Snowball crowded in, so Holly gave them carrots, too. She fed the last one to Plug. He nuzzled her pockets for more.

"All gone," she said. "Sorry."

Gently, she took hold of Magician's forelock—he didn't even need a halter—and led him into the barn. Only

Ragtime was inside. Angela refused to turn him out because then he'd get messy and she'd have to groom him. His stall was a disaster.

Magician's smelled fresh and wonderfully clean. Holly had stripped it the night before and put down two bags of shavings. She'd even removed all the cobwebs she could reach and had shuddered when the spiders scuttled for safety. Then she'd dusted off the windowsill because she wanted it to be as perfect as possible for Twiggy.

Giving Magician a handful of hay to keep him occupied, she got busy with a dandy brush. He'd gotten burrs in his mane again. As Holly was carefully pulling them out, her cell phone pinged.

Twiggy?

No, another email from "Misty." Same as before.

I.C.U.

Despite the heat, Holly shivered. She jabbed the trash icon so hard, the phone slipped from her sweaty fingers. Who *was* this girl? At least, Holly assumed it was a girl. No guy would ever call himself Misty. Magician nudged her. He was out of hay.

"No more," Holly said, digging her cell phone out of Magician's bedding. She flicked shavings off the screen. "We're going for a ride."

Ragtime whinnied.

For a mad moment, Holly was tempted to turn him

out—to let him enjoy being an ordinary horse instead of a hot-house plant. But Angela would have a bird. She'd stamp her feet and complain, and Mrs. Dean would threaten to fire Mom—the way she always did whenever Angela had a meltdown.

Not worth the risk.

Poor old Ragtime would have to stay in his stall, covered in a blanket and neck wraps. It wasn't normal; it wasn't right. Horses belonged outside in the fresh air. Even Olympic dressage champions like Valegro were allowed to frolic in their paddocks.

It was now six o'clock. In another half hour, Mom or Kate or both of them would be at the barn for morning feed. They'd wonder where Magician had disappeared to.

She'd better leave a note.

"Gone riding," Holly scrawled on the whiteboard in Mom's office. With luck, someone would see it before hitting the panic button.

* * *

It never got old, this incredibly wonderful feeling of having both legs wrapped firmly around her horse. Magician snorted and arched his neck, almost as if he knew how Holly felt.

While stuck in her wheelchair, she'd watched other girls compete on Magician and win the blue ribbons that she used to win. The docs had diagnosed Holly's paralysis as being "all in her head," triggered by the car accident that had killed her father. And, because of this, Holly's mind had put a lock on her legs. But another accident or traumatic event, so the docs said, might very well unlock them.

And it had.

Last year, a fire at the barn had forced Holly to walk again. She'd gotten out of her wheelchair to rescue a horse from burning alive.

Buccaneer.

Kate had loved him to bits. But after two months at Timber Ridge, he'd been sold on. Nobody knew where he'd gone until the previous month in England, when they'd bumped into him at a horse show being abused by the same trainer who'd abused Twiggy's horse. Would they ever see Buccaneer again?

Probably not.

Halfway down the road toward Timber Ridge Manor, where all the fancy houses were, Holly realized she'd forgotten to wear her helmet and swap her sneakers for paddock boots. Mom would have a fit—if she found out.

But if she turned back now, she'd run into Mom or Kate. They'd make her help with chores, and after that it would be too late to catch Twiggy on her own. Feeling guilty, Holly decided to keep going.

Magician shied at a brick mailbox. He'd seen it a dozen times before, but right now he was acting as if the mailbox had sprouted horns and teeth overnight.

"Silly boy," Holly said, laughing.

Ahead was Angela's house, a three-story McMansion with stone lions guarding the front door. Last Halloween, Kate had ridden up the Deans' driveway, hoping for a trick-or-treat donation to the horse rescue charity they were collecting for. The next day, Mrs. Dean had accused Kate of trampling her front lawn.

She hadn't.

It was Angela who'd done the damage, just to get Kate in trouble. But right now, Holly wasn't about to risk anything. Carefully, she steered Magician between rock walls and topiary trees, keeping well way from Mrs. Dean's elaborate flowerbeds that were covered with ugly red mulch. It was a long shot, hoping that Twiggy would be awake this early.

But she was.

When Holly reached the Deans' patio, Twiggy was sitting beneath a black market umbrella, sipping a giant mug of tea. She leaped to her feet and sent her chair flying backward.

"Holly?" she squealed.

A warm breeze teased wisps of blond hair from Twiggy's ponytail; her blue eyes shone. In another life, another setting, she'd have been the perfect cover model for a medieval romance novel. You could almost imagine a crown on her head, or a tiara, at least. She had that royal look—serene, in charge.

Somehow above it all.

It wasn't something she tried for. In fact, Twiggy hated all that stuff. But, as Holly had once pointed out, it was part of her heritage.

"You mean I can't help it?" Twiggy had said.

"Yup."

"Blech."

Still wondering if Twiggy was the same as she remembered, Holly pulled Magician to a halt, being supercareful to stay on the driveway. No way did she want her horse to trample Mrs. Dean's grass or her precious roses.

"Why didn't you text me?" she said. Might as well get it all out in the open.

Twiggy flashed a smile. "I did."

"Yeah, like from the airport." Holly jumped off Magician and patted his neck. "But zero, zip, afterward."

"My cell phone went dead," Twiggy said. "I asked Angela to text you about it." She faked a theatrical yawn. "And then I fell asleep, like right after supper. Poor Angela had to practically carry me up the stairs. I'm dreadfully sorry."

The time difference.

Holly remembered how jet-lagged they'd been when she and Kate had flown home from England, three days before their parents' wedding. No wonder Twiggy had crashed into bed. Holly double-checked her cell phone.

Had she missed Angela's text?

Nope, nothing from Angela about Twiggy. Not a word.

"I guess I didn't see it," she said, wanting to strangle Angela, who'd obviously ignored Twiggy's request and hadn't bothered to text Holly. But right now, it wouldn't be a good idea to slam the Deans. Not while Twiggy was at their mercy.

Twiggy grinned. "No worries."

There was no sign of a bodyguard, so Holly said, "Where's your watchdog?"

"She's arriving later."

"She?"

"Yeah, Dad hired a woman detective," Twiggy said. "Can you believe it?"

Holly didn't know what to say. The first time she'd met Prince Ferdinand, she'd bawled him out for not paying enough attention to his daughter. But Twiggy didn't seem to care, so Holly bit her lip. She looped Magician's reins over one arm and pulled Twiggy into the biggest hug ever.

The princess squealed. "Yikes!"

"Double yikes," Holly said.

Still holding onto Magician, they danced around the Deans' patio like two little kids let loose on a playground.

Beaumont Park, the *Moonlight* premiere, and the dumb pirates all faded into the background. This was the real deal.

This was, like, *right now*.

And Holly couldn't get enough of it. She hugged Twiggy even harder to make up for not being able to hug her yesterday. They were going to have so much fun together Holly could hardly wait for it all to begin.

Behind them, someone yawned. "Isn't this a little early for a reunion?"

"You're awake?" Holly said.

When was the last time Angela ever saw a sunrise? As far back as Holly could remember, Angela had never gotten up early enough to get her horse ready for a show and had always expected someone else to do it for her.

"Yeah, whatever," Angela drawled. She tossed back a wave of black hair and rubbed her pale blue eyes. They bored into Holly. "What time is it?"

"Too early for you."

Twiggy nudged Holly, then took Magician's reins, as if she sensed this was a good moment to intervene, to smooth things over.

Like she did in London.

That's how she'd been trained, as Holly had discovered just by watching her in action. Royals smiled, they shook hands, and they never showed their emotions in public—not with the press hanging onto their every word and ready to spread rumors that would set the Internet on fire . . . like what happened when reporters found out that Twiggy had been kidnapped.

"Can I ride Magician?" she said.

Holly looked at her. "Right now?"

"Yes," Twiggy said.

She wore cutoffs and sneakers. Holly didn't have a helmet or boots to give her. She hesitated, then figured, *Why not?* If nothing else, letting Twiggy ride Magician up and down the Deans' driveway would take the wind out of Angela's sails. The only fall-out would be Twiggy's bare legs. Stirrup leathers could be vicious, and she'd probably get major bruises. But knowing Twiggy, she wouldn't complain.

"Okay," Holly said.

Magician stood perfectly still while Holly gave Twiggy a leg-up. No need to adjust the stirrups. Their legs were exactly the same length. So were their fingernails and their blond hair, except Twiggy's was curlier and several shades lighter.

"Thanks," Twiggy said.

"Don't trample the grass," Holly warned.

"Viola won't mind."

"Who?"

"Mrs. Dean," Twiggy said. "She told me to call her Viola."

Viola?

Nobody ever called her that, not even Mom. Holly caught her breath as Twiggy bypassed the driveway and took off at a brisk trot across the Deans' back lawn, which spilled onto the Timber Ridge golf course. A couple of golfers trundled past on a cart. One of them waved at Twiggy, or maybe he was shaking his fist. She'd get in serious trouble if she rode onto the green.

Softly, Angela groaned. "No."

But her mother didn't seem to care.

She stepped onto the patio holding a cup of coffee, nodded toward Twiggy now trotting in circles on Magician, and said, "Oh, how lovely. Princess Isabel is having *such* fun." She turned to Angela and Holly, who was biting her lip, waiting for Mrs. Dean to explode when she realized her lawn was being systematically trashed. "Doesn't she ride well?"

Angela almost choked.

After cantering Magician in a perfect figure eight with a flying change in the middle, Twiggy trotted up. She slid off Magician and handed the reins to Holly. "Thanks, he's absolutely fab."

"Great," Holly said.

But inside she didn't feel great at all. In less than five minutes, Twiggy and Magician had turned Mrs. Dean's immaculate lawn into a plowed field, far worse than what Angela had done last Halloween and blamed Kate for.

Had Twiggy even noticed?

Did she think it was just fine and peachy to ride roughshod over people's gardens without a care in the world? Or was this her way of getting back at Angela for not texting Holly?

Mrs. Dean shrugged it off.

It was absolutely no problem, she insisted when Twiggy apologized. The landscape crew would fix it tomorrow.

6

"SHE'S OBLIVIOUS," Holly said, slamming Magician's saddle onto its rack so hard that her stirrups bounced. "Totally clueless."

"Who?" Kate said. "Mrs. Dean?"

"No, Twiggy." With an exasperated sigh, Holly ran her stirrups back up their leathers. "Aren't you listening?"

Kate tried to feign interest, but her mind was on other things—like the fact that she'd freaked out when Magician wasn't in the back paddock and that nobody had seen Holly's note on the whiteboard till they'd finished morning feed. Liz had been about to call for a search.

"Stupid, stupid," she'd muttered.

Luckily, Kate had persuaded Liz to go home for breakfast before Holly and Magician got back to the barn. Otherwise, there'd have been fireworks, *major* fireworks, mostly because Holly had ridden without a helmet and proper boots. Holly owed her for this one.

Big time.

But that's how it was with sisters. You covered each others' backs, even when you thought your sister was being a dope.

"Let's go swimming," Kate said. "We'll take the horses to Crescent Lake." She rummaged in her tack trunk. There was an old bathing suit in there, somewhere. "Twiggy could come, too. She can ride Rebel or Daisy, and we'll have a picnic on the beach."

"Can't," Holly said.

"Why not?"

"I'm having lunch at the club."

"Oh?" Kate waited.

Seconds passed—it felt like hours—until Holly finally shrugged. "I'm sorry."

In other words, Kate hadn't been invited. Holly and Angela and their royal guest would be having a gourmet lunch with Mrs. Dean at the exclusive Timber Ridge clubhouse. Tonight there would be a welcome dinner for Princess Twiggy. Members only.

And Kate wasn't a member.

But she would be, as soon as her father and Liz bought the house from Mrs. Dean. Feeling every kind of hurt imaginable, Kate gritted her teeth. Did she want to be part of Mrs. Dean's snooty social circle?

No way.

But apparently, Holly did . . . as long as Twiggy was in town.

* * *

At ten o'clock, Liz called for a riding team lesson, but Kate's heart wasn't in it. No matter how well Tapestry performed over the outside jump course, clearing fence after fence, Kate couldn't stop thinking about Twiggy. It didn't help that the princess was riding Rebel and doing it brilliantly.

"Great job," Liz called out.

Twiggy punched the air with her fist like a jockey who'd just won the Triple Crown. She'd improved a lot since the last time Kate had seen her ride. Lessons at Beaumont Park had made a huge difference.

For all of them.

Kate knew that she was a better rider—and so was Holly—for having been coached by Olympic stars like Will Hunter and Nicole Hoffman. They were Kate's idols. They'd already been where she wanted to go.

Liz raised the jumps, including the bar over the chicken coop that Tapestry loathed. In her previous round, Kate had avoided the coop, but now she couldn't. It sat there, like a malevolent pile of wood, waiting for her to totally flub up.

"You first," Liz called out, pointing at Kristina.

Her palomino gelding flew over the course as if he'd been doing it forever. So did Angela with Ragtime. Then came Holly and Magician.

They aced it—followed by Twiggy on Rebel. Jen's horse didn't put a foot wrong, and he threw in a small buck after they cleared the last jump. Maybe he'd been juiced up with vanilla pudding by the little kids who'd crowded around Twiggy, excited about having a princess at the barn. Kate had no idea. But whatever it was, she had to match it with Tapestry.

First up was the brush, then the crossrail. No problem. Tapestry jumped them with inches to spare. They made a gentle left turn and faced a simple oxer. One, two, three, Kate counted, and Tapestry soared over the red-and-white poles. Next came the in-and-out, which could be a challenge if you didn't pace yourself correctly. But Tapestry had no problem with those jumps, either.

"Good girl," Kate said.

Around the far corner they went, up and over the hogsback and then the parallel bars, followed by a double-oxer. They did a quick rollback and headed for the oxer again. Tapestry's hind foot clipped the top rail, but it didn't fall.

One more jump.

The dreaded coop. Kate tried to relax but felt herself tensing up as they cantered toward it. Enormous wooden chickens stood on either side in place of wings. The

Timber Ridge maintenance crew had made them for the end-of-camp horse show and now they were a permanent fixture.

Tapestry slowed. She swerved left and right, then dug in her toes so hard, Kate almost fell off.

"It's only a dumb coop," she said.

But Tapestry wasn't having any of it. Last year, when Kate first found her, Tapestry had been trapped in a field strewn with trash, junk cars, and scraggly chickens that pecked at anything that moved, including Tapestry's legs. Chickens—and their coops—were now the enemy.

Was anybody watching?

No, they were all clustered around Twiggy and Rebel. Even Liz, who should've been paying attention to Tapestry, was now focused on the princess. Gritting her teeth, Kate aimed for the coop again, faster this time. Tapestry faltered, but Kate kept her legs on, driving her horse forward with everything she had.

"Go, go," she said.

Just when it felt as if Tapestry would refuse again, she crow-hopped the coop. Kate let out her breath. They wouldn't win any prizes with a performance like this, but at least they'd gotten over the miserable coop. Kate hugged her mare.

"You're *my* princess," she said.

"Mine, too," said another voice.

At the fence stood Marcia Dean. She climbed onto the

top rail and swung her leg over it. She gave Kate a thumbs-up.

It wasn't a big deal.

Marcia was just a kid who loved Tapestry as much as Kate did, but right now Marcia's thumbs-up meant the world to Kate. Switching on a high-voltage smile, she trotted over to the little girl.

"Thanks," she said.

A year ago, this never would've happened. Back then, Marcia was a nondescript barn rat who'd been at Angela's beck and call. She'd scrubbed buckets, cleaned tack, and groomed horses for her demanding stepsister. On Angela's orders, she'd even waved her yellow windbreaker at a cross-country fence that Kate and Magician had been about to jump at last summer's Hampshire Classic. It had almost cost their team the challenge cup.

Despite her smile, Kate shuddered.

When she allowed herself to think about it, they were all a hair's breadth away from something unexpected—a blue ribbon you never thought you'd win, a horse getting stolen, or your brand new sister taking sides with a girl she'd always hated.

* * *

That afternoon, things got even worse when Holly's boyfriend showed up with Domino, his half-Arabian pinto. Adam had always stayed with Brad Piretti when hanging out at Timber Ridge, but now that Brad's family was no longer there, Adam had booked a room at a cheap motel on the other side of town.

But Mrs. Dean wouldn't hear of it. "You can stay with us," she'd said.

Oh, great.

That was all Kate needed. Another reason for Holly to spend every spare minute at Angela's house.

Feeling like a third wheel, Kate watched Holly fling her arms around Adam and drag him off to meet Twiggy. He hadn't seen her since they'd both been kidnapped by the pirates and spent two days tied up on a boat and then in a cave. Adam said he couldn't wait to hang out with Twiggy again.

"Hang, get it?" he'd said, yanking at his collar and pretending to choke.

Holly had punched him.

She was always doing this, and it struck Kate as kind of childish. One of these days, Adam would get fed up and punch her back.

But Aunt Bea disagreed when Kate told her what had been going on. She hadn't wanted to say a word, but Aunt Bea was really good at worming stuff out of you. It was, she claimed, how she got ideas for her stories.

"It's not Holly who's being childish," Aunt Bea now said, "it's you."

"Me?" Kate said.

They were sitting at the kitchen table. Liz was giving a dressage clinic at Fox Meadow Hunt Club, Holly had gone trail riding with Adam and Twiggy, and Dad was at his butterfly museum waiting for Kate to show up.

It was part of their deal.

He paid for Tapestry's upkeep in return for Kate working at the museum two half-days a week. She'd been about to ride her bike down to the village when Aunt Bea had sidetracked her by putting the kettle on and insisting they have a cup of tea.

"Yes, you," said Aunt Bea. "You're punishing Holly because she likes Twiggy. This isn't a crime."

Kate sniffed.

"You can be best friends with more than one person," Aunt Bea went on.

"We're not best friends." Kate took a quick gulp of tea. "We're sisters."

"And that makes it different how?"

"She's—" Kate began.

"—supposed to include you in everything she does?"

"Yes."

"Because you're now related?"

Kate nodded. "Yeah, I guess."

There was a pause. "Do you include Holly in everything you do?" Aunt Bea said. "Have you got a secret diary or a boy you like that you haven't told her about?"

Bing, bing.

How did Aunt Bea know about Kate's diary or her crush on Luke Callahan? Kate had never even admitted to herself how much she liked him. At the end-of-camp show Luke had praised Tapestry, and that had been enough to make Kate fall a little bit in love with him.

A crush. A silly, schoolgirl crush.

That's all it was, just like Holly and her friends who crushed on the latest pop stars and boy bands. But Kate hadn't told Holly—or anyone else—about liking Luke because she'd already been through all this celebrity stuff when she'd been dating Nathan Crane.

He was such a big star that they'd never been able to have a normal date without hordes of fans yelling and screaming and begging for autographs. At a local pizza joint, one girl had offered up her arm for Nathan to sign. It would be exactly the same with Luke Callahan.

No, Kate didn't want to go there again.

Not that Luke Callahan had even suggested it. He'd only admired her horse . . . but still, a girl couldn't help but wish and wonder, especially now that Aunt Bea was asking questions that made Kate squirm.

She fidgeted in her chair.

It felt as if all her deepest secrets had just come tumbling out and were now spread across the kitchen table for Holly's aunt to pick over like a bird pecking at worms on the front lawn.

"It's none of Holly's business," Kate finally said.

"Bingo," said Aunt Bea, sounding like a game-show host.

Kate flinched.

"You can have it one way or the other," Aunt Bea went on. "But you can't have it both ways. Either learn to respect each other's privacy, or—"

Kate's cell phone pinged. Dad wanted to know when she'd be at the museum. Astonished that her father actually knew how to send a text, Kate texted back:

On my way.

This was the perfect excuse to escape from Aunt Bea's eagle eyes and sharp nose.

* * *

Dad's van was in the museum's parking lot when Kate arrived. So was a yellow sports car she didn't recognize. It was pretty fancy for Vermont. Most people around here drove SUVs and mud-spattered trucks.

She leaned her bike against the sign for "Dancing Wings"—a Monarch butterfly wearing ballet slippers and a pink tutu. It had been put up by the museum's previous owners, and Kate always thought her dad would tear it down.

But he hadn't.

And now even Kate had to admit that the tacky sign did its job. People from all over—including entomologists and grad students—came to admire Dad's exotic butterflies and moths. His assistant walked out the front door as Kate entered.

"He's in a bad mood," Mrs. Gordon said.

"Why?"

"Somebody trod on a blue morpho."

"Is it dead?"

"What do you think?" said Mrs. Gordon. "The guy had a size twelve work boot." She gave an exasperated sigh. "That poor little butterfly didn't stand a chance and your father is beside himself." Mrs. Gordon was as batty about moths and butterflies as Dad was.

"I'm sorry," Kate said. Blue morphos lived in threatened habitats from Mexico to Colombia. The large, brilliant blue butterflies were getting harder and harder to find. "Maybe another one will hatch."

"We just have to hope," said Mrs. Gordon. She strode out to her car and maneuvered her angular body into the driver's seat.

Kate waited till she was out of sight, then went to find her father. He wasn't inside the glass atrium, which meant he was either tidying up the gift shop or squirreled away inside his messy office.

As she passed the museum's check-in desk, Kate straightened a stack of brochures and scooped a plastic tiara off the floor. A glittery pink antenna stuck out from each side, like something from a Disney princess film. Feeling kind of silly, Kate slipped the tiara onto her head.

With luck, it would make Dad smile.

She found him where she expected to, in his office, surrounded by books, papers, and scientific journals that spilled off shelves and onto the floor. But he wasn't alone.

The guy talking to her father had his back to Kate. Was he the one who'd trashed the morpho and was now apologizing to Dad or being reamed out by him? Kate checked his feet. Loafers, no socks. Definitely not work boots.

The visitor turned. "Hi, Kate."

7

HOLLY FELT GUILTY THAT KATE WASN'T WITH HER, but there wasn't a thing she could do about it. Right now, she and Adam were trapped in Mrs. Dean's living room, perched on the world's most uncomfortable sofa, while Twiggy seemed perfectly at home.

Well, of course, she was.

Her house in London was filled with priceless antiques—crystal chandeliers, Oriental rugs, and portraits of Twiggy's royal ancestors framed in gold. There'd even been a suit of armor beside the front door.

Mrs. Dean offered Twiggy another glass of iced tea. "When is your bodyguard arriving?"

"She just texted," Twiggy said, pocketing her phone. She stretched out her feet, clad in neon pink sneakers that matched her fingernails, and parked them on Mrs. Dean's coffee table. "She'll be here in a few minutes."

"Good," said Mrs. Dean. "We have dinner reservations at the club for six thirty." She glanced at Twiggy's feet, now dangerously close to an elaborate glass sculpture that probably cost a small fortune. "Maybe you'd be more comfortable"—she hesitated—"in proper shoes?"

"No worries," Twiggy said. "I'll change when my bodyguard gets here. We've got plenty of time."

Earlier, Mrs. Dean had announced that the bodyguard would occupy the room beside Twiggy's. They would share a connecting bathroom, and if they needed anything—fresh towels, soap, shampoo—they were to let her know immediately. She was at their disposal.

"What's her name?" said Mrs. Dean.

"Meredith Tudor."

"*Tudor*? Like King Henry?"

Twiggy shrugged. "I guess."

"Oh, wonderful," said Mrs. Dean. "Wonderful."

Holly had never seen Angela's mother so animated and happy. It was almost as if she were hugging herself over this. She poured even more iced tea for her royal guest and offered yet another round of cheese puffs. At this rate, they wouldn't need any dinner. But Mrs. Dean kept on smiling. She preened like a peacock.

She beamed at everyone.

But her face fell a few moments later when the door

bell rang and she opened the door to find a young black woman on her front step.

"Are you here about the job?" Mrs. Dean said.

Angela joined her mother at the door. "What job?"

"I told the agency to send over another maid, and she was supposed to go straight to the kitchen," said Mrs. Dean, clearly irritated. "I need help with our royal guest."

"That's why I'm here," the woman said. With a confident smile, she held out her hand. Her fingers were long and slender, and her nails had a flawless French manicure that Holly would've died for.

"Oh?" Mrs. Dean stepped back.

"I'm Meredith Tudor," the woman said. Her voice was low and clear, as if she were used to situations like this. "I'm a licensed bodyguard, and I'm here to protect your royal guest."

"B-but your name," Mrs. Dean stuttered, ignoring the woman's outstretched hand. "It's Welsh."

"Yes, I'm half Welsh," said Meredith Tudor.

"What's the other half?"

"American," she said and picked up a small suitcase. "Now, may I please come inside? I have a job to do." There was a pause. "Oh, and by the way, I carry a gun."

* * *

Kate blinked. She barely recognized him. His two-day stubble, the aviator sunglasses, and rumpled black jacket with sleeves rolled halfway to his elbows made him look older and far more sophisticated than Kate remembered. "What are you doing here?"

"Well, hello to you, too," he said.

His voice was exactly the same—deep, with the hint of a smile behind it. Nathan took off his sunglasses, and Kate was struck again by how much he looked like Adam.

"Hi," Kate said, feeling awkward. She sat down so hard, her tiara fell off. She kicked it beneath Dad's desk.

Nathan laughed. "Put it back on."

"Why?"

"Because it suits you."

The last time Kate had seen Nathan Crane was at the *Moonlight* premiere, where she'd told him to get lost for treating her like a toy that he could pick up and discard whenever he felt like it. After that, he'd gone to ground, but he'd surfaced later at the *Moonlight* party in London that Holly and Twiggy had been to. But this didn't explain why he was here—at Dancing Wings.

It made no sense.

Dad had met Nathan, briefly, at the premiere in New York, and he'd been puzzled afterward why Kate had dumped the famous movie star. Probably because she hadn't explained it very well.

Poor Dad.

He didn't get teenage girls—or anyone else, for that

matter. If you didn't have antennae, iridescent wings, and multiple eyeballs, you weren't on her father's radar. Well, except for Liz, of course.

Dad said, "I've got things to do, so why don't you two run along, and—"

"—grab a pizza?" Nathan said.

"Good idea," Dad said. He looked at Kate. "Save a slice for me, okay?"

"Sure," Kate said. "And I'm sorry about the morpho."

Dad shrugged—he wasn't nearly as upset as Mrs. Gordon had made him out to be—and said, "I have several cocoons. They'll be hatching next week."

"Oh, good," Kate said.

Nathan looked at her. "What's a morpho?"

"I'll explain later."

"Okay." Nathan stood. He shot her a goofy grin, then bowed and offered his arm like a movie star from years ago. "Shall we?"

This was beyond ridiculous, but Kate couldn't help herself. She no longer cared about Nathan as a boyfriend, but he was still a friend. His name had been linked with Twiggy's ever since they met at the party in London, so maybe that's why he was here—to see the princess.

Kate wanted to find out.

* * *

After Mrs. Dean bustled off and Angela had taken Twiggy and her bodyguard upstairs, Holly looked at Adam. "A gun?" she said.

"That's what PIs carry."

"PI?"

"Private investigator," Adam said.

Holly shuddered. Would Meredith Tudor be allowed to sleep in the guest room beside Twiggy's that Mrs. Dean had made such a big deal out of getting ready, or would she be consigned to a servant's room in the attic? Did Angela's house even have an attic?

And what about Mrs. Dean's dinner reservations at the club? She'd either cancel them or concoct a feeble excuse for not including Twiggy's new bodyguard.

"Let's get out of here," Holly said.

"How?"

"We just leave," Holly said.

No way was she going to be part of Mrs. Dean's prejudice. Last month, Angela's mother had been insufferably rude to a Native American chief over the alpine slide she'd wanted to build at Timber Ridge. It had ended badly—for Mrs. Dean.

Adam said, "I'm game."

They were halfway out the front door when Twiggy raced down the stairs, followed by Meredith Tudor. "We're coming with you."

"Where to?" Adam said.

Holly grinned. "Alfie's."

* * *

"I'm sorry for being a jerk," Nathan said over a sausage pizza with onions and extra cheese. It was Kate's favorite and they'd had it several times before, at this very spot.

Alfie's wasn't crowded—just a few locals who paid no attention to Kate and Nathan. They probably had no clue who he was, thanks to his sloppy disguise.

"It's okay," Kate said.

"No hard feelings?"

She shook her head. "None."

"What about Brad?" Nathan said. "Are you still seeing him?"

"He left."

"Why?"

Kate shrugged. "His family moved away."

"Is there anyone else?"

Nathan was even worse than Aunt Bea. Maybe he needed to know that she had another guy in her life so he wouldn't feel guilty over what had happened.

A waitress stopped by offering more soda. Kate covered her glass. "No, thanks."

"C'mon," Nathan said. "Tell me. Because if the guy doesn't like you, I will—"

Kate laughed. "What?"

"Run him over with my new car."

It was parked behind Alfie's, hidden out back where nobody would see it. The yellow Lamborghini must've cost an arm and two legs. Kate didn't know much about cars, but she could tell this one was crazy expensive.

Like off the charts.

For that kind of money you could buy an eight-horse van with luxurious living quarters, automatic waterers, closed-circuit TV, and toilets that flushed. On the other hand, she'd loved riding in Nathan's car with the top down and the wind in her hair. For two hours, they'd cruised the back roads of Winfield, laughing and talking about old times, and it was almost six o'clock when they'd gotten to Alfie's.

Nathan picked up a slice of pizza. Cheese dribbled down his chin and Kate had to resist the urge to wipe it off like she did with her father. She'd taken care of him ever since her mom died when Kate was nine.

Nathan said, "I have something to tell you."

"About the princess?"

"No, about me." Nathan looked at her, and his smile did that crinkly thing at the corners that made his fans swoon. Gone were the bags beneath Nathan's eyes, the tension lines around his mouth. There was no sign of the haunted look that had spoken of late nights and too much partying. "I'm quitting the film business and going back to school," he said.

This was the last thing Kate expected. Nathan's movie career had been like a shooting star. All bright lights and a brilliant future. Until, of course, it burned out.

"When?" she said.

"As soon as the next film is over." Nathan swallowed the last drops of soda and set his glass down firmly on the table, as if to make a point. "I'll do the *Moonlight* sequel, and then I'm off to the University of California—if they'll have me."

"What will you study?"

"Biogeography."

Kate had never heard of it. "What's that?"

"The study of the distribution of species and ecosystems in geographic space, and geological—"

"Stop," Kate said, laughing. "You sound like you're quoting from Wikipedia."

Nathan grinned. "I am."

"Is this because of New Zealand?"

"You got it," he said. "Those caves were amazing."

While on location last year in the mountains of New Zealand, he'd sent Kate dozens of photos—pictures of rock formations in remote places that hardly anyone knew about and tunnels that went for miles underground, filled with rare bats and creatures that never saw the light of day. Dad had probably been quizzing Nathan about this when Kate had shown up.

As if reading her mind, he said, "I asked your father for advice."

"And did he give it?"

"The eminent professor told me to study whatever got my heart started."

"Caves and bats?"

"Yes," Nathan said. "And did you know that bats have the most amazing metabolism? They can digest bananas, mangoes, and berries in about twenty minutes."

This was like listening to Dad. "You're obsessed," Kate said. "And I love it."

"But will the princess?"

"Twiggy?"

"Who else?" Nathan said.

The door banged open. Holly, Adam, and Twiggy burst into Alfie's like a tidal wave, followed by a woman Kate had never seen before. Twiggy waved.

Kate stiffened. "Ask her yourself."

* * *

After Nathan and the princess got through hugging one another, Adam dragged over another table and four more chairs. Why were they here instead of at the club? Kate decided not to ask—at least, not right now. Then Holly introduced Twiggy's new bodyguard and Kate couldn't help feeling that she'd heard the name before.

Meredith Tudor.

It rang a dozen bells, but none of them made a clear connection. Meredith Tudor wore jeans, a crisp white shirt, and a denim jacket. There was a slight bulge on one side, just beneath her left arm. Was that a gun or Kate's imagination?

Aunt Bea would love this.

More pizza arrived, along with two jugs of soda. Across the table, Holly chatted with Nathan, pretty much ignoring Kate, while Adam and Twiggy were trying to outdo one another with stories about their kidnapping adventure.

Meredith Tudor listened attentively.

Hardly surprising, given it was her job to protect Twiggy. But what had Meredith Tudor done before she'd become a bodyguard? That was the question that was bothering Kate. She hated it when she recognized a name yet couldn't place it.

Nathan invited Holly for a spin in his new car. He circled the block a couple of times, then drove back for Adam. Off they went, roaring down Winfield's main street faster than they needed to. Kate hoped they wouldn't get a ticket. The village only had one cop, but he was vigilant about teenagers and speeding. The gossips would grumble.

That jumped-up movie star is driving around town in a car that costs more than most people's houses.

But Nathan wasn't worried, because by the time that happened, as he'd already told Kate, he would be on his way to Romania to begin shooting the *Moonlight* sequel.

Kate agreed with the gossips.

Nathan's car didn't belong in Winfield. Not when most people worked two jobs to keep a roof over their heads. Trouble was, Nathan knew what it was like. He'd grown up in Vermont, and he'd been Adam's best friend until Hollywood had turned his life upside down.

Did this happen to all the stars?

Would it happen to Kate if she got good enough and famous enough to ride the Grand Prix circuit? Would wealthy sponsors fall all over themselves to offer her million-dollar horses to compete with? Amid thoughts of riders like Ineke Van Klees and Luke Callahan, Twiggy's voice brought Kate down to earth with a bump.

"My turn," the princess squealed as Nathan and Adam came zooming back. With their windblown blond hair and matching aviator sunglasses, you couldn't tell which one was which.

"Not so fast," said Meredith.

Twiggy turned to her. "Huh?"

"This is a two-seater," she said. "There's not enough room for me."

"No worries," Twiggy said. "You go first with Nathan, and I'll go afterward."

"That's not the point," said the bodyguard. "You're not going off in a car by yourself." She glanced at Nathan, then back at Twiggy. "And I don't care how famous he is."

Adam handed Meredith the keys to his truck. "You can tail them."

"I've got a better idea," she said, handing them back. "You drive, and I'll ride shotgun."

Twiggy laughed, then jumped into Nathan's car and told him to floor it. Airily, she waved at her bodyguard, and Kate wondered how long it would be before Twiggy figured out a way to spring herself loose. Probably longer than Twiggy thought. Meredith Tudor looked as if she'd been around the block a few times and wouldn't be easily fooled by a headstrong princess, no matter how devious she was.

"Meredith's way cooler than Stephan," Holly said, the moment Nathan and Twiggy drove off. Belching smoke, Adam's old truck trundled behind the Lamborghini like Marmalade lumbering around the paddock trying to keep up with Magician.

"Who?"

"Twiggy's old bodyguard."

Kate had never met him. She followed Holly back inside the restaurant, relieved that Holly had actually spoken to her. Did this mean their feud, or whatever it was they'd had, was now over? You didn't always know with Holly. Her mood was sometimes hard to read.

The others would be gone for a while, so maybe this was a good time to sort things out. Kate sat down opposite Holly, knowing that if she sat beside her, Holly would only shift over.

"So," Kate said. "Why aren't you talking to me?"

"I just did."

"I mean talking, like *really* talking. Not just saying stuff."

"Stuff?"

"Yes," Kate said. "You've been ignoring me ever since Twiggy arrived, and I'd like to know why." She took a sip of soda. It had gone flat, pretty much the way this conversation was about to go.

"Oh, get real," Holly said.

With a sigh of exasperation, she pulled out her cell phone and began to scroll, idly flicking through screens as if already bored. Kate was about to try again, when Holly gasped. She put a hand to her mouth, then looked up, eyes huge and frightened like a deer caught in headlights.

8

HOLLY'S BLOOD RAN COLD. Her hands shook so hard she could barely read her phone. Right there, on the barn's Facebook page, was Misty.

Hi, Holly. Miss me? LOL. Get it? MISSty me!

No photo—just a cartoon of a fat blond princess wearing a lopsided crown and riding an equally fat pony. A dozen thoughts flashed through Holly's mind, all of them bizarre and off-the-wall crazy.

Princess . . . crown . . . *pony*?

Could this be Twiggy, or was it Angela, messing with Holly's head? No, no, on both counts.

Twiggy would never do anything like this, and Angela wasn't savvy enough to set herself up with an anonymous Facebook account or even e-mail, for that matter.

"What's wrong?" Kate said.

Holly gulped. She couldn't even breathe. In a flash, Kate was beside her. She felt Kate's firm hand on her back, pushing her down.

"Put your head between your knees," she said.

"Why?"

"You're having a panic attack."

"Me?"

"Yes, you. Now shut up and bend over."

Holly bent, sucking in one shallow breath after another, but it wasn't enough. She was suffocating. It was like being trapped inside a wet sleeping bag with no way to get out.

"You all right, miss?" said the waitress.

"She'll be fine," Kate said.

Their voices sounded far away, muffled. Holly concentrated on breathing. In and out, in and out. It couldn't be *that* hard. It was what she'd done every day of her life without even having to think about it. After what seemed like hours, but was probably only a few minutes, things returned to normal.

"Phew, that was scary." Holly sat up, feeling dizzy. She held onto Kate for support. "How did you know I was having a panic attack?"

"A girl at my old stable used to have them before a big class," Kate said. She handed Holly a glass of water. "Drink this."

"Thanks," Holly said.

Her phone was lying face up on the table with Misty's message in full view. Holly reached for it, but Kate got there first.

"Who's Misty?"

"Nobody." Holly felt herself turn red.

"Liar," Kate said. "It's that girl, isn't it?"

"What girl?"

"The one who's been following you."

Holly bit her lip. She didn't want to talk about this, because if she did it would all become horribly real. She'd have to admit that she was a little bit freaked out, not totally in charge of her life the way she liked to be. Tears welled up. Quickly, she wiped them away but not before Kate noticed.

"C'mon," she said. "I'm your sister, remember?"

That was the trouble. If she told Kate, then Kate would insist they tell Mom and Ben or go to the police. And what would Winfield's cop do? Put out an all-points bulletin on a skinny blonde with two-inch nails? Holly was madly searching for an excuse—anything would do—when the others returned, all talking at once. This was enough to distract Kate, so Holly snatched back her phone and stuffed it into her pocket. Out of sight, out of mind.

For now, at least.

"Hey," Twiggy said, throwing herself onto a chair beside Holly. "That car is a total blast." She shoved a chunk of tangled blond hair behind one ear. "But I broke a nail, see?" With a dramatic sigh, the princess thrust a hand in front of Holly. "I hope there's a decent nail salon around here."

Holly stared at Twiggy's neon pink nails. They weren't two inches, but—

No, that was loony-tunes.

Totally crazy.

Besides, Twiggy hadn't even been in Winfield last week when Kate insisted they were being followed.

* * *

The moment they got home, Kate confronted Holly. "Okay, spill."

"I can't."

"Try," Kate said.

She knew how incredibly tough this was for Holly. She'd made a career out of being strong, of brushing off her two years in a wheelchair as if it were nothing.

But Kate knew better.

She'd watched Holly churn up and down the backyard pool, hour after hour, strengthening her arms and shoulders while her legs trailed uselessly behind. Almost every day, she'd helped Holly with exercises that had gone nowhere, including the therapeutic riding lessons that Holly hoped would help her to walk again.

But nothing had worked—until the fire that almost

killed Buccaneer. Kate shoved him out of her mind. This was about Holly, not a horse that neither of them would ever see again.

She climbed into bed.

The black-and-white pony that Holly had given her the other night lay on her pillow. Kate picked him up and hugged him. His fluffy fur tickled her nose and she wished she'd had a stuffed pony like this. It would've helped during those long, lonely nights after her mother had died and Dad had retreated into his office, leaving Kate to cope on her own. After another fierce hug, she tossed the pony back to Holly.

"Your turn," she said.

It took a while and Kate could hear Holly wrestling with her pony print comforter and adjusting her numerous pillows. Books were opened and closed; stuffed ponies got exuberantly hugged and tucked into a nest that surrounded Holly.

Patiently, Kate waited.

* * *

Holly caught her breath. This was hard—harder than talking about her stupid legs when they wouldn't work. But this stalker stuff? Was it all in her head, like the docs said that her paralysis had been? Was she getting paranoid?

No, absolutely not.

This was real. She had not imagined the e-mails from

Misty or the Facebook post because she'd read them. With a sigh, Holly climbed out of bed and dropped her cell phone onto Kate's lap.

"See for yourself."

Even though she'd deleted Misty's e-mails, they were still there, buried in the trash. You couldn't get rid of them without blowing up your phone or tossing it out and getting another one with a different number. Right now, Holly wanted to blow up Misty, whoever she was.

After a moment, Kate sighed. "Okay, what now?"

"I don't know." Holly slumped onto Kate's bed.

At least Kate hadn't said they should tell Mom and Ben about Misty—or the police. This was definitely a plus. For a moment, neither of them spoke and it was as if all the issues they'd had over the past week had suddenly vanished.

Poof.

. . . vanished like that blue ribbon you desperately wanted to win that landed on another horse's bridle, or like a case of colic that disappeared the minute you called the vet.

"I'm sorry," Holly said.

"Me, too."

Holly flung herself back onto her own bed, then got up again, too restless to lie down. She gathered up all her ponies and kissed each one in turn. "So, what should we do?"

"Get help."

"Like who from?"

Kate frowned. Her brow crinkled the way it always did when she was thinking hard. "Aunt Bea?"

"She'll tell Mom."

"How about Mr. Evans, then?"

He was Aunt Bea's special friend, and Holly adored him. So did Kate. He'd given her a stall for Tapestry at his dairy farm last February when Mrs. Dean had thrown them out of Timber Ridge. "Nope," Holly said. "He'll tell Aunt Bea, and then—"

"I've got it," Kate said. "I know exactly who we can ask."

"Who?"

"Meredith Tudor," Kate said. "She's a detective."

"No, she's a PI," Holly said.

"Stop splitting hairs," Kate said. "Meredith's a professional. This is her job. She'll know what to do."

"Yeah, right," Holly said, having second thoughts. If she told Meredith—or anyone else for that matter—about the stalker, they'd laugh and tell her she was being silly, that she was making mountains out of molehills. Still hugging her ponies, Holly paced the floor. There wasn't much room and she tripped over a pile of magazines. A *Young Rider* went slithering beneath her bed.

"Sit," Kate said. "You're making me nervous."

"I'm the one who should be nervous, not you." Holly

said. "You're not being stalked by a blonde with killer nails."

"Hah!" Kate said, sounding triumphant. "So you *do* believe me, then."

Holly hesitated. "Yes . . . no."

"Do you have any suspicions?" Kate said. "Like who'd want to stalk you?" She was starting to sound like an interrogator.

"No, I mean, yes. I think so."

There was a very long pause. Then Kate said, "Is it the princess?"

"Don't be an idiot," Holly snapped. "Twiggy wasn't even here last week."

"Okay, so how about Angela?"

"She's not a blonde."

"She was last year," Kate said. "Remember?"

How could either of them forget? Last summer when parts of *Moonlight* were shot at the barn, Kate and Angela had both wanted the stunt-double role. The day before their screen tests, Angela had appeared with blond hair, just like the actress they'd be doubling for. Desperate to win the part so she could buy a horse, Kate had dyed her hair blond, only to discover that Angela had been wearing a wig. In the end it hadn't mattered because the character in *Moonlight* had black hair.

Poor Kate.

Not only had she looked like a complete idiot in front

of everyone, she'd had to live with six months of bad-hair days. Even now, the tips of her long brown hair were still tinged with gold.

Could it be Angela?

With a sigh, Holly straddled her old wooden rocking horse. Most of the paint had worn off and its stringy mane needed a wash. One of its ears had gone missing. She began to rock, back and forth. Not only did it soothe her, it helped to get her sluggish brain moving again, to look at the facts.

Angela was obviously hopping mad because Holly had run off with Twiggy and left Angela behind. But was she mad enough to post that message on Facebook? She'd have had plenty of time, providing she'd been able to figure out how to get herself an anonymous Facebook account.

But this didn't explain how Angela knew about Misty. Unless, of course, it really *was* her.

Holly shuddered.

Was Angela Dean the bottle blond with two-inch nails Kate had seen at the Sugar Shack?

9

Slowly, Kate opened her eyes. The room was bright, too bright. She blinked as sunlight streamed through the window.

What time was it?

In the other bed, Holly was still asleep, flat on her back with a tangle of sheets around her ankles and covered in stuffed ponies. They'd stayed up way too late, arguing about the stalker and getting absolutely nowhere.

They'd also forgotten to set the alarm.

Kate leaped out of bed so fast she almost fell over. Her clock said nine forty. "Holly, wake up," Kate said, shaking her.

Holly moaned. "Go away."

Yawning, Kate rummaged for the clothes she'd abandoned the night before. No, those wouldn't do. She needed breeches and a clean t-shirt. The one from yesterday had pizza stains down the front. And where had she left her riding boots?

Five minutes later, Kate staggered into the kitchen. Aunt Bea was at the table, trying to butter a piece of toast with one hand. She glanced at Kate. "Rough night?"

"Ugh." Kate leaned against a chair.

"What's wrong?" Aunt Bea's nose wrinkled, as if she suspected something. Kate knew her guilty face would give it away, so she busied herself with pouring cereal and milk into a bowl. She ate, standing at the counter, her back toward Aunt Bea.

But it didn't fool Holly's aunt.

"Something's up," she said. "But I won't push. If you need to talk, I'm always here." There was a pause. "Well, for the next day or so. Then I'll be going home."

"Is your arm better?"

Aunt Bea patted her sling. "This comes off tomorrow."

Did this mean Holly would insist that Twiggy and her bodyguard leave Angela's house and move over here instead? Kate hoped not. She and Holly were finally getting themselves sorted out. Having Twiggy around, like *all* the time, would mess it up.

Kate choked down the last of her cereal. It was almost ten. There was a riding team lesson in twenty minutes. They'd never make it on time. Tapestry had probably rolled, and Magician would have a bazillion burrs in his mane. Plus Kate hadn't cleaned her tack yesterday. She'd been planning to do it this morning before the lesson. Fat chance of that now.

"I gotta run," she said.

Holly burst into the kitchen, pulling her hair back into a messy ponytail. Her paddock boots were unzipped, her pink t-shirt was inside out, and if Kate wasn't mistaken, Holly was wearing a pair of Kate's old breeches she'd been meaning to throw out.

"Mom's gonna kill us," Holly said, as she headed for the door. "We're late."

"What about breakfast?" said Aunt Bea.

"No time."

"Then eat this." Aunt Bea handed Holly her toast. "You can't ride on an empty stomach."

"Thanks," Holly said, scattering crumbs.

Kate grabbed two carrots from the fridge and followed Holly out the back door, straight into a wall of heat.

"Yikes, it's hot," Holly said.

As they ran past the swimming pool, Kate was tempted to jump in, clothes and all. She was already sweating buckets, and by the time Liz got through with them, she'd be sweating even more. Maybe she'd even melt. The sun was high in the sky, promising another scorcher.

"Hold up," Holly said.

Kate almost ran into her. "What?"

"Over there, look."

Whipping off her sunglasses, Kate squinted toward the barn. Two horses were trotting circles in the outdoor ring—a dark bay and a flashy chestnut with a long, flowing mane. "Is that Twiggy?"

"Yup," Holly said. She had better eyesight than Kate. "She's on Rebel, and they're doing great."

"So, who's riding Ragtime?"

"Angela?"

"No way," Kate said. "Angela can't ride like *that*."

"But she never lets anyone else ride him," Holly said. "Not even Mom. He's totally off limits, so it's got to be Angela."

"Not this time," Kate said.

Ragtime's nose was tucked, his neck arched, and his hindquarters more engaged than Kate had ever seen. He looked like a different horse.

She took a few steps closer.

Okay, so who was this mysterious rider getting half passes and flying changes out of Angela's expensive Dutch warmblood? A new student? Another instructor to help Liz? Or—Kate gulped—someone to replace her?

* * *

Holly couldn't take her eyes off Ragtime. Ears pricked, Angela's bay horse extended across the diagonal with feet that barely seemed to touch the ground. His rider sat deep in the saddle. She wore tan breeches, brown gloves, and a pale blue polo shirt. Her boots looked old and creased; her helmet was dusty. As they turned the far corner, Kate grabbed Holly's arm.

"Is that Meredith Tudor?" she said.

"Looks like it." Holly let out a low whistle. Twiggy's father had insisted on a bodyguard who could ride, and Holly had pegged Meredith as a casual trail rider—maybe even Western—but not someone like this.

Kate said, "She's a dressage star."

"No kidding," Holly said as Ragtime swung into a collected canter that would've scored a perfect ten on a grand prix test.

"No, really," Kate said. "I recognized her name but couldn't place it."

"So why haven't I heard of her, then?" Holly didn't pour over *Chronicle of the Horse* and *Dressage Today* the way Kate did, but surely she'd have heard about an African American dressage rider, especially one as good as Meredith Tudor.

"Because she dropped out of sight four years ago," Kate said.

Holly snorted. "When you were eleven?"

"Yes," Kate said. "I read magazines then, too, you know."

"That's because you're a geek," Holly said, still watching Ragtime. On a loose rein, Angela's horse mouthed his double bit, and flecks of foam flew onto his sweaty shoulders. This happened with Angela, especially after she'd stressed him out. But Ragtime didn't look stressed now. He looked relaxed, ears swiveling like antennae, and ready for his rider's next signal.

Twiggy trotted up. "Isn't Meredith amazing?"

"Totally," Holly said. "Did you know she was this good?"

"Nope," Twiggy said. "But I do now." Sliding off Rebel, she staggered about, pretending to collapse. "My legs are killing me. Meredith put me through the wringer and I'm totally knackered."

Holly wasn't sure what *knackered* meant. Something British, probably. Twiggy was always coming out with stuff that nobody understood. At least, nobody on this side of the Atlantic. Yesterday, she'd said that Nathan's car was absolutely "dench."

"Like the actress?" Holly had said. She only knew about Judi Dench because of Mom. She watched British sitcoms every Saturday night on Public TV, and you were in big trouble if you interrupted her.

Twiggy had shrugged. "I guess."

By this time, Meredith and Ragtime had disappeared into the barn. Holly wanted to follow and fire off questions, but then Mom came out and told them to get moving. She and Kate had five minutes to catch their horses, groom them, and tack up.

* * *

Kate put Tapestry on the crossties while Holly led Magician into his stall. Moments later, Twiggy was there, offering help.

"Thanks." Holly handed Twiggy a hoofpick and grinned when the princess gave Magician a kiss on his nose. "How's Diamond?" she said. "I hope you've got pictures."

"Dozens," Twiggy said as she loosened a clump of dirt from Magician's hoof. "I'll show you later, but—"

"What's wrong? Is he okay?"

"Diamond's fine." Twiggy bent over to pick out another hoof. "It's Buccaneer I'm worried about."

"Why?"

Twiggy straightened. She ran her hand down Magician's hind leg and when he didn't pick up his foot, she leaned into him. "He's off his feed, and I think he's lost weight."

"Give him more Life Savers, then," Holly said. "They'll fatten him up."

"Caroline says he misses Kate."

"Oh, that's crazy," Holly said.

But was it? When Buccaneer was at Timber Ridge last summer the only girl he'd let ride him was Kate; he'd barely tolerated Mom on his back. And, after they'd rescued him from Vincent King, Kate was the only one who'd ridden him at Beaumont Park.

"Even Will Hunter has problems with Buccaneer,"

Twiggy went on. Gently, she shoved Magician to one side. "And he dumped Nicole Hoffman in the dressage arena last week. It was a perfect hit. She landed right on top of the letter M."

"Poor thing," Holly said. "Is she all right?"

"She's fine," Twiggy said, finishing off her last hoof. "But I'm afraid that poor old M has turned into N and a wonky I."

"You're joking."

"Just a bit," Twiggy patted Magician's rump. "He looks just like Buccaneer, doesn't he? I bet Diamond would love him."

"Why?"

"Because Diamond adores Buccaneer. He won't go anywhere without him. They've got adjoining stalls, and the last time we went to a show, Diamond wouldn't load onto the trailer until Buccaneer went inside first."

"They're not gonna sell him, are they?" Holly said. Beaumont Park was a world-class training barn. Horses that didn't work out got sold on.

"They wouldn't dare," Twiggy said, eyes twinkling. "He's Diamond's best friend and my father—"

"Hurry up," Kate yelled. "Liz is waiting."

Holly wasn't even tacked up yet. "Don't tell Kate," she whispered, hefting Magician's saddle onto his back. "She'll get her knickers in a knot if she thinks Buccaneer is unhappy."

* * *

After a grueling session with Liz that involved endless gymnastics without their stirrups, Kate cornered Twiggy in Rebel's stall. "Where's Angela?" she said.

"Home, sick."

"Yeah, right," Kate said.

More than likely, Angela was faking it. And Kate didn't blame her. She wouldn't want to be in Angela's shoes right now, coming to the barn and looking like an idiot in front of everyone, all because her mother had behaved atrociously about Meredith.

Not that she hadn't before. Mrs. Dean was always making a fool of herself. But she ruled the roost and nobody—not even Liz—had the power to override her. Well, except for the Homeowners' Association, and they seemed to be letting Mrs. Dean get away with whatever she wanted these days.

"No, honestly," Twiggy said, brushing the dried sweat off Rebel's broad back. His muscles twitched. "Angela threw up this morning."

"Bummer," Kate said. Even though she didn't like Angela, throwing up was the pits. "Did she tell Meredith to ride Ragtime?"

"Not really. But I'm sure it's okay," Twiggy said airily.

But Kate had her doubts.

Like Holly said, Twiggy was oblivious. She'd been here

just over twenty-four hours, and trouble with a capital T had already found her. First she'd trashed the Deans' back lawn, then she'd blown off Mrs. Dean's welcome dinner, and now she'd just helped herself to Angela's horse without asking permission.

Three strikes.

No four. She had Meredith Tudor as a bodyguard, and Kate could easily imagine Mrs. Dean's reaction to that. Would it send her over the top? Would Princess Isabel and Meredith Tudor be kicked out of Castle Dean?

Twiggy dropped her brush into Jennifer's grooming box and snagged a hoofpick. For someone who'd never taken care of a horse or cleaned tack before going to Beaumont Park, she'd certainly come a long way.

Kate thawed a little.

Maybe it wouldn't be too bad if Twiggy and Meredith came to stay with them. Especially Meredith. Kate would give anything to pick her brains.

Four years ago, Meredith Tudor had been about to become the first African American to ride for the U.S. Olympic team when she'd suddenly disappeared. Nobody knew why—not even the *Chronicle*. Kate had only been eleven when it happened, so she hadn't questioned it—not back then.

But she did now.

What was it that had stopped Meredith's riding career in its tracks? An accident? Getting dumped by her sponsors? Or was it an evil trainer like the one Twiggy and Angela had?

* * *

Mrs. Dean arranged another party for Twiggy. "Tomorrow night, at the club," she told an astonished Liz. "It'll be a barbecue, and I've invited lots of other horse people, so you must join us and bring your lovely new husband and your daughter." There was a significant pause. "And Katherine, of course."

Katherine?

Holly almost choked. Nobody called Kate that unless they were mad at her. Then again, Mrs. Dean had been mad at Kate ever since she'd arrived at Timber Ridge last summer.

But Kate didn't want to go. "Why should I?"

"For me?" Holly said.

"You'll have Adam—and Twiggy," Kate said. "You don't need me as well."

"What about Meredith?" Holly said. This would get Kate's attention. Ever since ten thirty that morning, when they'd seen Twiggy's bodyguard riding Ragtime, Kate had been desperate for more information about the mysterious dressage rider. "This'll be your best chance. You'll probably be able to get her all to yourself."

"*If* Mrs. Dean invites her," Kate said.

Holly grinned. "She will."

"How do you know?"

"Twiggy texted her dad and told him to call Mrs. Dean." Holly's grin grew wider. "Apparently, Prince Ferdinand made it quite clear that wherever Twiggy went, Meredith was to go as well. End of discussion."

"Good for him," Kate said.

"So you'll come?"

"Yeah, but I've got nothing to wear."

"That's *my* line, not yours," Holly said, laughing.

But in Kate's case, it was perfectly true. Apart from a couple of thrift-store bargains that were now destined for the trash, the only dresses Kate owned were the pink bridesmaid's dress she'd worn for their parents' wedding and a blue chiffon gown that Holly had made her buy for the premiere in New York, neither of which were suitable for a summer barbecue at the club.

Was it time for another makeover?

And would Kate go along with it? She had last year for Mrs. Dean's Labor Day party and her Hawaiian luau at the club's indoor pool when they'd both worn leis and tie-dye sarongs. Kate had even let Holly do her hair and makeup—a hint of blush, a dusting of eye shadow, and just enough lip gloss to convince Kate that she wasn't only a horse girl . . . she was a *real* girl.

But a new dress was out of the question. Neither one

of them had any money. They'd have to find something in Holly's half of their overstuffed closet. Holly flung open the door.

"Here, try these," she said, tossing a peasant skirt and an embroidered blouse toward Kate. This wasn't Holly's style, but it'd look fine on Kate. So would these tan sandals. They had a bit of a heel, but with practice, Kate would be able to walk in them.

Next came Holly's turn.

She pawed through her closet, discarding one outfit after another. A rainbow of clothes flew about until Holly pounced on a scarlet dress with spaghetti straps and a bias cut skirt.

Perfect.

Triumphantly, she hugged it to herself and twirled in front of her full-length mirror. The skirt rippled around her knees. "How about this?"

Kate shrugged. "Looks fine to me."

"As if you'd know."

* * *

On Sunday morning, Holly went trail riding with Adam. Kate waved them off and wished she had someone special to go trail riding with. Brad had come close. He'd taken lessons from Liz, and he'd tried hard to fall in love with horses, but Kate knew that deep down his heart had belonged to the football field and the Timber Ridge half-pipe.

You couldn't force it.

You either loved horses, or you didn't. Or you loved them because you loved all animals, but you didn't love them enough to do all the work involved.

With a sigh, Kate reached for a broom. She swept the aisle and tidied up the tack room, then grabbed a pitch-fork and mucked out Tapestry's stall. Magician's stall was a mess because Holly hadn't had time to clean it, so Kate took care of it for her. She cleaned Domino's stall as well.

The barn was quiet.

Even the cats were asleep, having spent the night chasing mice and whatever else it was that kept them occupied. Liz was in the indoor arena, giving lessons to the boarders—middle-aged women who'd decided to recapture their youth by riding horses again. A couple weren't bad; the others were predictably awful.

But it made Kate think.

Would this be her in twenty-five years? Would she be one of the hopefuls circling a bored instructor, desperate to win blue ribbons at the next adult hunter-jumper show?

No, absolutely not.

If Kate's Olympic dreams didn't work out, she'd go to college. She'd have a career, and—

The barn door slid open.

Marcia and Laura bounced inside. Their fresh faces, their freckles, and their unbridled enthusiasm knocked Kate for a loop. This was what it was all about—having fun with your horse, not obsessing over blue ribbons.

"Hey, Marcia," Kate said. "You want to ride Tapestry?"

"You bet," Marcia said.

Kate went to get her saddle and Rebel's, too. She still hadn't figured out how to deal with Mr. Dean's offer to lease Tapestry.

Was it a good idea?

Or would it send her Olympic hopes into freefall?

10

NONE OF THE OTHER GIRLS had boyfriends at Mrs. Dean's barbecue. Angela had just broken up with Channing Alexander, Twiggy was pretending she didn't miss Nathan, and Kate was off in a corner talking to Meredith Tudor.

Feeling kind of special, Holly stood beside Adam. He'd already charmed Mrs. Dean and was now regaling her with stories about how he and Twiggy had been abducted by pirates. Angela's mother was enthralled—or pretended to be.

"Really?" she said. "How did you escape?"

While Twiggy chimed in with her own version, Holly took in their surroundings. The club's patio had been transformed into fairyland with a bazillion lights that glittered along pathways and twinkled from trees and umbrellas. A floodlit waterfall tumbled over fake rocks into the swimming pool; half a dozen fountains sprayed pink and blue water. Edging closer, Holly sighed with relief as the cool mist hit her face.

"You'll get wet," Adam whispered.

She grinned. "I don't care."

Her stomach rumbled. She glanced toward the barbecue, where two chefs in white aprons and tall hats were grilling an assortment of ribs, hot dogs, and interesting looking stuff on skewers. A waiter drifted by with canapés. Holly snagged two stuffed clams and offered one to Twiggy.

She eyed it suspiciously. "What's this?"

"A clam."

"Littlenecks," Adam said, helpfully. "Steamers and quahogs."

"*Mercenaria mercenaria*," added Kate's father. "Once used by the Algonquians to manufacture wampum."

"Yikes," Twiggy said, taking a small bite. "I don't think we've got these in England." She wrinkled her nose. "We've got cockles and mussels and—"

"—alive, alive-oh," trilled Mrs. Dean.

Everyone stared at her.

Where had that come from? Holly had no idea. It sounded really old fashioned, like something her grandmother used to sing. But Mrs. Dean was smiling, and that was always a plus.

"I love that song," Twiggy said.

"Liar," Holly whispered.

"Shut up," Twiggy whispered back. "I'm trying to be nice."

More guests arrived. Mrs. Dean, still smiling like the Cheshire cat, exclaimed over each one, making such a fuss you'd think George Morris and the entire U.S. Equestrian Team had just shown up. Finally, the crowd thinned and Holly caught her breath. Was that Luke Callahan walking toward them?

* * *

Kate was finding it easier than she'd expected to talk to Meredith Tudor. At first, she'd been a bit tongue-tied, the way she always was with people she didn't know. But Meredith had a friendly smile and she was happy to answer questions.

But not the one Kate had just asked.

"It's complicated," Meredith Tudor said, smoothly sidestepping the issue of what had ended her dressage career. "Why don't you tell me about your horse?" She steered Kate to the buffet table. "I've always loved chestnuts, especially when they've got flaxen manes and tails. What breed is she?"

"Morgan," Kate said and was about to explain how she'd rescued Tapestry from the kill truck, when someone tapped her shoulder. She whirled around. A bacon-wrapped scallop flew off her plate and landed at Luke Callahan's feet.

"Sorry," he said, bending to pick it up. "I didn't mean to startle you."

Kate opened her mouth and closed it again. She felt herself turn red. Instinctively, she put a hand to her face. Was her mascara running? Had she bitten off all her lip gloss? What about her hair? The upswept style Holly had talked her into was probably a tangled mess by now, given how hot and humid it was out here.

Her peasant skirt itched.

If only she were wearing cutoffs and sneakers, she'd have felt a whole lot more comfortable inside her own skin. Holly's sandals were killing her.

After giving Luke a curt nod, Meredith melted into the crowd, and Kate found herself alone with show jumping's teenage superstar. He quirked an eyebrow and looked at her, as if waiting for a reply.

"Hi," she said.

Boy, that was totally lame.

"You're Kate, right?" he said.

She nodded.

"Thanks for being so cool with my sister."

Sister?

For a second or two, it didn't compute. Then Kate remembered Charlotte, a sweet little girl who'd been at the horse camp with her Norwegian Fjord and how Angela had called the horse a dump truck in front of Luke.

"She's a great kid," Kate said.

Another lame remark.

Why couldn't she talk to people, especially guys, as easily as Holly did? Her sister was across the patio, chatting with Adam and Luke's father as if it were the most natural thing in the world—never mind that Sam Callahan was a big-name trainer who wrote articles for the *Chronicle* that Kate obsessed over.

He was tough on his students, and even tougher on his daughter. Because of his constant criticism, Charlotte's self-confidence had gone down the tubes, and when Kate discovered why, her hero worship of Sam Callahan had dimmed a little. Out of nowhere, a hidden sound system struck up a pop-rock number.

"Wanna dance?" said Luke Callahan.

With a lopsided grin, he brushed back a lock of brown hair. His eyes were bluer than the swimming pool, and Kate wanted to jump into them.

She looked around. "Me?"

"Sure," he said. "Why not?"

But before Kate had a chance to gather her wits, Angela sidled up. She wore a strapless yellow sundress with a slit up one side, and her cheeks glowed with good health. There was no sign of whatever it was that had made her too sick to ride yesterday.

"Luke," Angela said, purring like a kitten. "You promised me the first dance. Remember?"

With an apologetic look at Kate, Luke Callahan allowed himself to be dragged onto the dance floor by a girl he was supposed to hate.

* * *

"I don't believe it," Holly said, shaking out her ponytail and tying it up again. "You let Angela steal him?"

"He wasn't mine."

"Oh, poof," Holly said. "Of course, he was. Luke asked me where you were, and I told him. Besides, he loathes Angela. Remember how she bad-mouthed his sister's pony?"

"Horse," Kate corrected. "Norwegian Fjords are horses, not ponies."

"Semantics," Holly retorted.

They were in the club's lavishly decorated women's room—marble sinks, crystal chandeliers, and carpets thick enough to get lost in. Wall-to-wall mirrors surrounded them.

Kate scowled at her reflection. "I thought *you* liked him."

"I do," Holly said. "I think Luke Callahan is totally awesome, but I've got Adam." She swiped on a layer of mango lip gloss. "And you need another boyfriend."

"Do not."

"Luke's perfect for you," Holly said.

"Yeah, right," Kate said, looking gloomy. "Me and a million other girls."

Holly switched gears. There was no point in trying to get Kate to talk about Luke, or any other boy for that matter. They were off her radar, up in the clouds somewhere, as scary to Kate as spiders were to Holly.

"What did Meredith say?"

Kate shrugged. "Nothing much."

"Did you find out what happened to her?"

"She said it was complicated."

"That's all?" Holly said.

"Yeah."

The door opened part way, and Twiggy's head appeared. "Hey, you guys. We've got cake."

Inwardly, Holly groaned. She couldn't eat another thing, not after the bruschetta and all those clams she'd scarfed down, and that plate full of barbecued ribs she'd shared with Adam.

The moment Twiggy disappeared, Kate said, "What's Sam Callahan doing here?"

"Mrs. Dean invited him."

"Why?"

Holly hesitated, unsure if this was a good time to tell Kate that Mrs. Dean wanted the Callahans to buy a house at Timber Ridge. She decided to hold off. Besides, it was probably a rumor—or wishful thinking on Angela's part.

Even though Luke had blown her off at the horse-camp show, Angela still seemed determined to get her hooks into him.

* * *

Mrs. Dean had pulled out all the stops for Twiggy's cake—a Disney castle festooned with pink rosebuds, silver stars, and a skinny blond doll on top wearing heels and a tiara.

"Barbie meets Tinkerbell," Holly muttered.

The cake decorator had misspelled Twiggy's name. "Welcome, Princess Isabele," it said in a flowery script. Holly grabbed a spoon and carefully removed the last *e*.

But Twiggy didn't seem to care. With a goofy grin, she plunged her knife into the cake, scattering silver stars and pink frosting all over the table. People cheered. Others raised glasses of champagne.

Kate said, "Where's Angela?"

"She was here a minute ago," Holly said, looking around. But there was no sign of her. "Maybe she's gotten sick again."

"Yeah, right," Kate said.

From across the patio, Holly caught Luke's eye. Kate hadn't noticed that he'd been looking at her ever since he'd extricated himself from Angela. He grinned and gave Holly a thumbs-up, then walked toward her. *So, okay, how did you tell a cute guy you barely knew that your sister was a total doofus?*

"Don't interfere," Adam warned.

Holly punched him. "What would you know about it?"

"Lots," he said. "I've had a good teacher."

Holly raised her fist again, but Adam laughed and fended her off. Then he kissed her cheek. They'd only been dating for a year, but it felt as if they'd always known one another, never mind that Adam lived fifty miles away, rode for Larchwood, and went to a different high school.

But he was right.

She mustn't get involved. Kate and Luke would find each other, or they wouldn't. There was nothing Holly could do about it, short of throwing them together in a closet and locking the door.

Something sparked. The music screeched to a halt, and all the lights went out with a pop. Holly fumbled for her cell phone. She was about to turn on its flashlight, when the fairy lights flickered and came back on again. Mrs. Dean tapped her glass with a spoon.

"A temporary glitch," she announced.

"Like last time?" Kate muttered.

Holly didn't even want to go there. Last November, Angela had ruined Holly's fifteenth birthday party by dousing the lights and pulling the fire alarm. The sprinklers had soaked all the guests and wrecked Holly's cake before she'd even had a chance to cut it. Mrs. Dean had blamed the club's manager, but Holly knew it was Angela.

Would she try the same trick again?

Not even Angela was that stupid. And no way would she mess up her mother's party for Twiggy. No, it had to be someone else.

The stalker?

That was even more ridiculous. How would a stranger get into the club and know where to find the circuit breaker box or whatever it was that controlled the lights?

No, this was an inside job.

Which brought Holly back to Angela. Maybe she really was dumb enough to pull another stunt like this.

11

HOLLY WOULDN'T LET THE POWER FAILURE GO. Finally, Kate tuned her out and fell asleep, too tired to argue. The next morning, Holly brought it up again.

"All this proves," Kate said as they walked into the barn, "is that it wasn't Twiggy."

"How?"

"Because she was standing next to me when the lights went out."

"So was Luke," Holly said.

"What's that supposed to mean?"

"Did he kiss you?"

"Don't be an idiot," Kate said, feeling herself turn red. If they ever invented a magic switch that would stop blushes, she'd be first in line to buy it.

Holly pounced. "Ah, so you *do* like him."

Kate ignored her. She didn't want to think about Luke Callahan right now, not when they were about to have a dressage lesson with Meredith Tudor. Liz had managed to talk her into it, with the proviso that Angela and Kristina were not included.

"Why?" Twiggy had asked.

"Because they'll blab it all over town," Holly had said.

And so would Mrs. Dean, Kate now thought as she slipped into Tapestry's stall. If Angela's mother did a search on Meredith Tudor and discovered that she'd mysteriously dropped off the dressage world's radar, she'd waste no time digging up the dirt.

Whatever it was.

Last night, as the party was winding down, Kate had tried asking Meredith again, but she'd politely changed the subject. Even Twiggy had gotten nowhere. Maybe her father knew, but if he did, he wasn't saying either.

* * *

By eight thirty, they were in the indoor, warming up along the rail. With a hand to her mouth, Meredith looked thoughtful as she assessed her three riders. She had them transition to a trot, back to a walk, and into a working canter. Then she called them into the center of the ring.

"You've all got good basics," she said.

Twiggy smiled. "Thanks to Beaumont Park."

"And here," Meredith said. "Liz is a great teacher. But

you could use a little fine tuning." She patted Rebel's neck. "Let's start with your reins. Move your fingers around. Play with the contact you have with your horse's mouth. It doesn't take much."

"Like this?" Twiggy said.

"Yes," Meredith replied. "But lower your hands."

As Meredith lengthened Holly's stirrups and adjusted Tapestry's noseband, Kate wondered how old she was. Twenty-five? Thirty? It was hard to tell. This morning's quick search on Google and the *Chronicle* had turned up the same old results that Kate had seen before. It was as if Meredith Tudor had ceased to exist after she'd quit competing.

* * *

For twenty minutes, they worked on half halts and going smoothly from a trot into a walk. "It's all about your seat," Meredith said.

"Mine's killing me," Twiggy grumbled.

Meredith smiled. "You can have a bath with Epsom salts later, okay? Now, immediately after your half halt, you must sit into the walk. Your seat should resist any more trot movement." She looked around. "Am I being clear?"

"Yes," Holly said.

"Once your horse knows to expect the change from your seat," Meredith went on, "he will switch his legs to a walk when he feels the signals that your rear end is giving him. Make sense?"

"I think so," Kate said.

There was so much to remember, and things got progressively more complicated as Meredith worked them through transitions from trot to canter. Inside leg, outside rein. More half halts. They'd learned a lot of this from Liz, and even more at Beaumont Park. But having Meredith reinforce it was like frosting on the cake.

"Now, let's ask for impulsion," she said.

After another twenty minutes, Kate was dripping wet, and all she could think about was diving into the pool. But Meredith kept them at it. Finally, when Kate didn't think she could take any more, Meredith said, "You've done a great job, so cool your horses off. Hose them down. They've earned it."

As if reading Kate's mind, Holly invited Twiggy and Meredith home for a swim. No need to waste time getting their suits and towels from Angela's house.

"We've got plenty of extras," she said.

Meredith wiped a hand across her sweaty face. "Sounds good to me. I could use cooling off, too."

* * *

Armed with flippers, masks, and a bunch of colorful noodles, Holly organized a relay race—her and Meredith against Twiggy and Kate. The first two swimmers would put on their flippers, leap into the pool, and swim like mad for the other end while bashing their opponent with a noodle. The more bashes, the better.

"Then what?" Kate said.

"You take off your flippers, put on the mask, and swim back under water," Holly said. "All the way—no surfacing—so hold your breath really well. Then your teammate does the whole thing in reverse."

"I'll never remember," Twiggy wailed.

Meredith grinned. "Sounds worse than a dressage test."

And off they went.

Twiggy bashed Meredith so hard, her pink noodle broke. Then one of Meredith's flippers came off, and she had to dive down to get it. Neither of them managed to swim all the way back without coming up for air.

But Meredith's flipper fiasco had given Kate a head start. She sucked in her breath and dived in. The pool wasn't long—forty feet or so—except she hadn't secured her mask properly and it slipped around her neck, which really cramped her style.

Holly caught up.

In no time, she swapped her mask for flippers and noodles and was totally merciless to Kate on the way back. Halfway home, they collapsed in a fit of giggles. Twiggy cannonballed into the pool. Seconds later, so did Meredith.

"Who won?" Twiggy said, gasping.

Meredith splashed her. "We all did."

While Holly tried to teach Twiggy the butterfly, Kate flopped onto a chaise beside Meredith. She'd begun to feel more comfortable around Twiggy's bodyguard. With all the craziness, it was like she'd become one the girls. Well, almost.

"Your sister is amazing," Meredith said, as Holly churned up and down the pool like a dolphin. "How did she learn to swim like that?"

Knowing that Holly wouldn't mind, Kate told Meredith about Holly's paralysis, how she'd kept herself fit by swimming, the fire that almost killed Buccaneer, and how it had forced Holly to walk again.

"She's got a lot of guts," Meredith said. "And it makes you realize how fragile, how temporary, life can be." A wistful look crossed her face. "You never know what's going to happen next—a bad fall, someone getting sick, or—"

Was Meredith going to open up?

But Twiggy ruined the moment. "Did you see me?" she cried, dripping water all over Kate. "I did the butterfly."

"Really?" Kate said. "I thought you were drowning. I was about to jump in and save you."

Twiggy flipped Kate with a wet towel and folded herself into a chair. Reaching into her bag, she pulled out her cell phone, then gave a dramatic sigh.

"What's up?" Kate said.

It was probably nothing. Twiggy was always sighing and acting like a drama queen. Her molehills didn't just become mountains; they turned into the Rockies or the Alps—the Himalayas, even. But she made it sound like fun, and you always wanted to find out what new trauma had befallen her, never mind if it was off-the-wall crazy.

"Dad left a message," Twiggy said, frowning. "I'd better ring him."

While Twiggy waited for her father to answer, Kate thought about the first time she'd seen the prince. He'd stormed down to Beaumont Park after Twiggy was kidnapped so he could lay the blame at Holly's innocent feet.

Prince Ferdinand was enormously tall, so Holly had climbed onto a footstool. Nose-to-nose with Twiggy's furious father, she'd accused him of making Twiggy's life miserable by abandoning her at a horrible boarding school and saddling her with an evil trainer because he didn't care enough to pay attention.

She'd even prodded him in the chest.

Twelve hours later, after they'd rescued Twiggy and Adam from the pirates, they'd seen the prince again in Twiggy's hospital room. Gone was the bluster, the self-righteous bully. Prince Ferdinand was now a very grateful prince, a deflated and humble prince.

Afterward, Holly had said, "Just like Tigger."

"When he got de-bounced after getting lost in the Hundred Acre Wood?"

They'd slapped each other a high five because they both adored Winnie the Pooh and because Twiggy was going to be okay, and Kate was still thinking about all this when Twiggy gasped. Her face had turned pale beneath its tan.

Meredith said, "Is something wrong?"

"No—I mean yes." Twiggy scrambled to her feet and grabbed Kate's arm. "I need help," she whispered. "Right now."

* * *

Holly climbed out of the pool in time to see Twiggy dragging Kate into the kitchen. "What's up with them?" she said, toweling herself off.

Meredith shrugged. "Twiggy talked to her father and—"

"—had a meltdown?"

"Pretty much."

"It happens all the time." Holly shook out her hair and showered Meredith with water. "Oh, sorry."

"No problem."

"I'll go and see what's wrong."

Luckily, Meredith didn't follow, which was a good thing. You never knew what would happen next with

Twiggy. Most of what she freaked out over turned into nothing more than hot air. Her father was probably causing a royal fuss because Twiggy had ignored his last e-mail or she'd blown a hole in her credit card.

But this was a lot more serious.

Kate hit her with it the moment Holly stepped into the kitchen. "Twiggy's dad wants to fire Meredith."

Holly sat down hard on a chair. "Why?"

"Guess."

"Mrs. Dean?"

It all tumbled out. Twiggy's words came so fast and furious that it was hard to keep up. Holly caught her breath as reality engulfed her like a big bucket of water. Somehow, Mrs. Dean had dug up Meredith Tudor's secret.

"She nobbled a horse," Twiggy said.

"*Nobbled*?" Holly said, ready to strangle her. "Speak English, would you?"

"It *is* English," Twiggy snapped. "It means doped. You know, giving horses drugs to make them perform better."

"I don't believe it," Kate said.

"Neither do I." Twiggy looked close to tears. "But—"

"—your father does," Holly finished.

"He told me to sit tight," Twiggy said, sniffing. "I'm not to say a word to Meredith. He'll get a replacement bodyguard from the agency, and if that doesn't work out, he'll fly Stephan over."

"Can he ride?" Kate said.

Twiggy looked at her. "Are you serious? Stephan doesn't know one end of a horse from the other."

"Neither does Mrs. Dean," Holly said.

* * *

"Now what?" Kate said, the moment Twiggy and her bodyguard left. Twiggy had done her best to look cheerful. They'd all agreed not to warn Meredith, even though Twiggy wanted to, despite her father's orders.

"I bet she's been framed," Holly said, shucking off her towel and jumping into the pool. She surfaced, spouting water. Holding her nose, Kate jumped in as well. Holly challenged her to a race.

"No fair," Kate said. "You always win."

"So try harder," Holly said.

"Why?"

"Because it will stimulate your brain, and maybe you'll come up with something useful to help Meredith." Holly rolled her eyes. "And you might even beat me."

Kate seriously doubted it. She'd never beaten Holly before, and she didn't this time, but thrashing up and down the pool in Holly's wake helped to put things in perspective.

Was Meredith Tudor innocent? Had she been framed like Holly suspected? If so, what on earth could they do to prove it? This wasn't a Nancy Drew mystery; this was real life. They couldn't sneak about like amateur sleuths with spy glasses and deerstalker hats.

Oh, wait. That was Sherlock Holmes.

"I've got it," Holly said. "I know exactly who to ask."

Kate almost slammed into her. "Who?"

"Sam Callahan."

"Luke's father?"

"Who else?" Holly said, treading water. "Do you know another Sam Callahan?"

"No," Kate said, and climbed out of the pool. The sun was still beating down on them, but life had suddenly gotten colder. Shivering, she wrapped herself in Holly's old Scooby Doo beach towel.

"So, what's wrong with my idea?" Holly said as she backstroked toward the deep end.

Kate hadn't shared her mixed feelings about Sam Callahan with Holly. Yes, he was a famous trainer, and, yes, he wrote amazing articles in the *Chronicle*. But he'd also traumatized his daughter to the point where she was too scared to jump a simple crossrail. And last night at the barbecue, Meredith had reacted strongly to seeing Luke. It wasn't much, but it added up.

Holly's cell phone pinged.

"Want me to get it?" Kate yelled.

"Yeah," Holly yelled back. She did a perfect flip turn, then dog paddled toward Kate. "It's probably Twiggy."

But it wasn't.

Kate listened, horrified, as a shrill voice threatened to turn Holly's life upside down.

12

To Kate's surprise, Holly shrugged it off. "She's an idiot."

"No, she's scary."

"That, too," Holly said, drying her hair. "But we've got other things to worry about." She pulled on a faded pink t-shirt with *Barn Bratz* written across the front. "I'll deal with Misty later."

"You're being pig-headed."

"Am not," Holly said. "I'm being pragmatic. There's nothing we can do about stupid Misty, but there *is* something we can do about Meredith."

"Like what?"

"I don't know," Holly said. "But we'll figure it out."

"Sam Callahan?"

Holly gave a little shrug. "Bad idea."

"Yeah," Kate said, relieved that Holly had already abandoned it. Luke Callahan's father was the last person they should ask.

But the rest of it was an act.

Deep down, Holly was scared, but she'd never let on. She pretended to be invincible, always in charge, and never letting stuff freak her out—or admitting to it. But that was dangerous because if you did that, when really bad stuff happened, you weren't equipped to ask for help.

You were too proud.

Or you were too scared to admit that you were scared. Kate pulled her sister into an awkward hug. After a second or two, Holly disentangled herself.

She sniffed. "Thanks."

"Okay," Kate said, sounding more confident than she felt. "Let's look at this logically. First of all, how did Mrs. Dean find out that Meredith was a dressage rider?"

"Angela told her?"

"She didn't know," Kate said. "And neither did Kris. She wasn't around the day Angela got sick, remember? Nobody knows about Meredith except you, me, and Twiggy." She heard a car door slam, which meant that Liz was back from taking Aunt Bea to the doctor. "And your mom."

"Should we tell her?"

Kate shook her head. "Not till we do some digging."

"So where do we start?"

"Angela's cell phone."

Holly stared at her. "Why?"'

"Because we won't be able to get our hands on Mrs. Dean's."

"I don't get it," Holly said, looking puzzled. "What would—?"

"Think about it," Kate said. "We might find a message or something on Angela's phone that would tell us how her mother found out about Meredith."

It was such a long shot that Kate felt kind of ridiculous for even suggesting it. But it would prove, one way or another, if Misty really was Angela in disguise. And no matter what Holly said, this was just as important as finding out who'd framed Meredith, or even if she'd been framed at all.

"That's sneaky," Holly said. "I don't like it."

"You got any better ideas?"

Holly sighed. "No."

"So, let's go," Kate said.

She figured that Angela would be at the barn right about now, and with luck she'd be riding with Kristina in the outdoor ring or on the hunt course. And maybe, just maybe, Angela would've have left her cell phone in the tack room—the way she often did—because it caused an ugly bulge in the pocket of her skin tight breeches,

And Angela hated that.

* * *

Holly spotted it first, hidden beneath a dusty curry comb inside Angela's even dustier grooming box.

"You keep guard," Kate said, "while I look."

Of course, Angela's cell had a four-digit password, and Kate hit gold the first time she tried. Angela's birthday.

How stupid was that?

Kate sucked in her breath. It freaked her out to be sneaking about like this. But if they were going to nail Holly's stalker and get to the bottom of Meredith's mystery, it had to be done.

How much time did she have?

There'd been no sign of Angela in either of the riding rings. She had to be on the mountain somewhere.

"Hustle," Holly said from the tack room's doorway. "Someone's coming."

Kate heard a whinny, the distant clatter of hooves. "Is it Angela?"

"I think so."

This meant she'd be here, dumping her saddle and bridle in just a few minutes, because she never bothered to rub down her horse after a ride. Kate looked around. She had two choices—put Angela's phone back where she'd found it, like right away, or take it with her.

No, that wouldn't work.

It would take Angela less than five seconds to figure out that her phone was missing, and the first person she'd accuse of stealing it would be Kate. And this time, she'd be right.

"Yikes," Kate said. "Can you stall her?"

"I'll try."

Madly, Kate scrolled through Angela's phone. Text after text slid by, but nothing that identified her as Misty. She pulled up Angela's Facebook page, but found nothing there either.

Okay, so it wasn't Angela.

In a way, Kate felt relieved. She really hadn't wanted Angela to be the stalker. But, just to make sure, she clicked on the message icon again. Somewhere, a horse neighed. It sounded like Ragtime. Quickly, Kate took a last look at the screen. A message she hadn't seen before scrolled by. Her mouth dropped open. *From Angela to Kris*, it read.

M in big trouble. C told Mom she doped a horse.

In the aisle, voices erupted. It sounded as if Holly were trying to stall Angela with a stupid joke they'd all heard a million times before.

Without thinking, Kate stuffed Angela's phone into her back pocket. And just in time, because two seconds later, Angela sailed through the door and dumped her tack on the floor, just like Kate knew she would. Almost immediately, Angela rummaged through her grooming box.

"Okay, where is it?" She glared at Kate, then at Holly,

lounging in the doorway and looking as if butter wouldn't melt in her mouth. "Who stole my phone?"

Holly raised her arms. "Search me."

Angela took a step toward her, and that was all it took. By the time Angela realized she was on a fool's errand, Kate had shoved Angela's phone back in the box, tucked beneath the same dusty curry comb that hadn't been used in weeks—months, probably. Quick as a snake, Angela found her phone and looked at its screen. A puzzled look crossed her face.

Kate swallowed hard.

Had she forgotten to hit the "home" button? If so, this meant that Angela's incriminating text message was still on her screen. It had all been such a blur, Kate couldn't remember.

* * *

"It doesn't matter," Holly said when they were well clear of Angela and the barn.

Kate kicked at a clump of dirt. There were lots of clumps of dirt between here and the house and she wanted to kick all of them. "I messed up."

"You didn't."

"Oh, yeah?"

"Get real," Holly said. "You proved that Angela isn't Misty and that Mrs. Dean has shafted Meredith."

"But we don't know who blew the whistle."

"C," Holly said.

"That could be anyone," Kate replied, stubbing her toe on a rock. It hurt almost as much as that dumb tooth she was trying to ignore.

"Like who?" Holly said.

Kate flexed her jaw, and the pain subsided. It was probably tension. "Angela's cousin, Courtney, or even her ex-boyfriend."

"Channing Alexander?"

"Why not?"

"Because he's not smart enough," Holly said. "And besides, he doesn't know one end—"

"—of a horse from another," Kate finished.

They stomped into the kitchen, grabbed two sodas from the fridge and a bag of potato chips off the counter, and continued their argument in their bedroom. For a horrible moment, Kate worried that Luke's sister, Charlotte, had pointed the finger at Meredith, but that was insane.

Charlotte was ten years old.

Okay, so how about dad's assistant, Cecilly Gordon? But she knew even less about horses than Mrs. Dean did.

Another name popped into Kate's head. Caroline West—Jennifer's grandmother, who owned Beaumont Park in England. No way would she be involved in something like this.

"We're not thinking properly," Holly said, tossing the chips to Kate.

The bag yawned open and crumbs flew all over the floor, adding to the mess that was already there. Kate's lips puckered as she bit into a stack of salt-and-vinegar chips. Her tooth twinged. She ignored it.

But Holly was right.

They weren't on the right track. Kate ran through all the other names she knew that began with C and came up empty. Maybe it was someone she didn't know, but Mrs. Dean did—someone in the horse world who held a grudge against Meredith Tudor.

An influential someone who could—

"I've got it," Kate cried.

She sat up so fast, her chips went flying across the room like pieces from a jigsaw—a puzzle she'd just solved. Well, almost. They'd been looking in all the wrong places. C wasn't a first name, it was—

"What?" Holly said.

"Callahan," Kate said and immediately hated herself.

"We've got to tell Mom."

"Yes," Kate said, hating herself even more.

* * *

Without interrupting, Liz sat quietly at the kitchen table while Kate and Holly told her what little they knew about Meredith.

"So," Liz said, taking a sip of her lukewarm coffee. "This is a surprise, I must say."

"You don't believe it, do you Mom?"

"Meredith wouldn't dope a horse," Kate said. "She's far too—"

"Nice?" Liz said.

"Yes."

"Kate, I'm afraid that nice people sometimes do bad things," Liz said. "We don't know Meredith, not really. We just know she's a fabulous rider, and from what you've told me, it sounds like she's an awesome instructor as well."

Holly looked around. "Where's Aunt Bea?"

"I dropped her at home."

"Is she all right?" Kate said. "Her arm is better?"

"More or less," Liz said. "It's healed enough so she can drive her car again."

"Good," Holly said. "This means we've got our spare room back."

"Holly!"

"I didn't mean it that way," Holly said, backtracking madly. Why did she always say the wrong thing? "What I mean is, we can have Twiggy and Meredith here, right?"

"That won't solve the problem," her mother said. "Twiggy's father is going to fire Meredith whether she's here or at the Deans'."

"Then we'll just have Meredith."

"Sounds to me like you don't want her to leave Timber Ridge."

Holly shook her head. “I really like her, Mom.”

“So do I, but we can’t interfere. We know nothing about this situation. And listen to me, both of you.” Liz looked sternly from one to the other. “The last thing I want is for you girls to charge off and take matters into your own hands. Do you hear me?”

“Yes,” Kate said, nodding.

Holly crossed her fingers and sat on them. Then she nodded as well, to cover herself. She’d just had the best idea in the world, and she couldn’t wait to share it with Kate.

There *was* something they could do.

But they’d have to be supercareful because if Mom found out, she’d ground them, like, forever.

13

"THE VERMONT CLASSIC?" Kate said, when Holly explained her plan about confronting Sam Callahan at a horse show. "It's fifty miles away. How are we going to get there?"

"Meredith will drive us."

"With Twiggy?"

"Of course."

"What about Angela?" Kate said. It was clear that Holly hadn't thought this all the way through. "She'll want to come with us."

"I know," Holly said. "So how do we stop her?"

"We can't," Kate said.

Stopping Angela was like trying to stop a runaway horse or a hurricane. Whatever she wanted, she got. Just like her pushy mother did. As for the Vermont Classic, it was one of New England's biggest equestrian events—six A-rated shows, back-to-back, one after another. It had been going on for most of the summer, and Superstar Luke had already cleaned up in the junior jumper division. He was on track to make a killing in adults, too.

"Sam Callahan?" Holly prompted. She sounded almost gleeful that her first idea, the one Kate had shot down, was now their only option.

"How are we going to find him?" Kate said. "This show is huge. It'd be like looking for—"

"—a needle in a haystack?"

"Worse," Kate muttered.

"Wrong," Holly fired back. "Sam Callahan is a judge, not a competitor, so we'll know exactly where to find him."

"Then what?" Kate said.

"We dig out the truth."

"How?"

"We *ask* him," Holly said.

"Seriously?"

"No, we tie him up and torture him," Holly said, rolling her eyes as if Kate were too stupid to live.

Kate gave a little sigh. They'd never get within fifty feet of Sam Callahan. He'd either be judging classes or in the VIP tent having a gourmet lunch. He wouldn't be hanging around the warm-up ring or eating overpriced hot dogs, waiting for a couple of teenage girls to give him the third degree.

* * *

That night, Holly managed to convince her mother that they needed to go to the Vermont Classic because Twiggy was desperate to see a real American horse show. "They're very different in England," Holly pointed out. "Twiggy's never seen a hunter equitation class."

This was a stretch, but luckily Mom was too distracted to notice. The annual Homeowners' Association meeting was tomorrow afternoon, and she had to present a report. It also got Mrs. Dean out of their hair.

Things were falling neatly into placc.

The prince hadn't yet found a replacement bodyguard, Twiggy hadn't said a word to Meredith, and neither had Mrs. Dean. She just pretended that Meredith didn't exist. The only fly in the ointment was Angela.

She'd insisted on coming, too.

I couldn't think of a reason to stop her, Twiggy had texted earlier. *Sorry*.

Holly adjusted her nest of ponies and snuggled into bed. Kate was already asleep. She'd been kind of quiet through dinner. Her tooth had flared up again.

"You must call the dentist," Mom had said. "Because if you don't, I will."

Hurriedly, Kate had agreed to make an appointment, but Holly knew she wouldn't. They had too much going on. Kate insisted that her tooth would have to wait till they solved the Meredith mystery.

It was kind of exciting—almost like a Nancy Drew book. A couple of them were propping up Holly's bed because the floor was uneven. Holly bent down and pulled out a copy that wasn't being used as a prop.

Blowing off the dust, she began to read.

* * *

Something woke Holly at dawn. For a few seconds, she lay perfectly still, listening to rain lashing her bedroom window. In the distance, thunder rumbled. Was that what had woken her up? Then she heard it again. A soft groan.

"Kate?" she said. "Are you all right?"

No answer.

Holly stumbled out of bed, tripped on a laundry basket, and landed in a heap beside her sister. Kate groaned again, louder this time.

"What is it?" Holly said, shaking her gently.

"My tooth," Kate mumbled. She tried to sit up. "It's killing me."

"Move your mouth," Holly said, "like you did yesterday."

Kate held her jaw. "Aspirin."

There was a bottle in the bathroom. Holly grabbed it and filled a glass with water. Kate swallowed two pills.

"Better?" Holly said, as thunder rumbled again.

She didn't want this to be happening, not today. In less than two hours, they had to get on the road with Meredith and Twiggy—and, oh horrors, Angela—so they could drive through rotten weather to the show grounds and find a place to park before eleven o'clock. That's when Sam Callahan would begin judging. After that, he'd be knee-deep in green hunters, pony riders, and anxious parents wanting to know why their kids didn't pin.

Somehow, they got through breakfast, but Kate was as pale as a sheet. She could barely keep her eyes open, let alone eat her cereal. Mom wasn't up yet, so Holly took over.

"Go back to bed," she said. "I'll manage."

"You can't."

"Oh, yeah?" Holly said. She loved a challenge, but not at Kate's expense. "And call the dentist, okay?"

Kate muttered something unintelligible and shuffled off. Holly had never seen her so sick. Maybe she had a fever. Maybe that stupid tooth was infected. Well, whatever it was, there was no way Kate was coming to the horse show. Holly and Twiggy would have to handle it by themselves.

* * *

Meredith's windshield wipers could barely keep up with the rain. It was like driving through a waterfall. Holly looked out the side window as town after dreary town flashed by, shrouded in mist and gloomy silence.

Even Twiggy was quiet. She sat behind Meredith, nose buried in the Nancy Drew book that Holly had found the night before. Angela, thank goodness, had decided not to come.

"She's afraid she might shrink," Twiggy had said.

At least the rain had been good for something, if only to keep Angela away. Holly checked her phone. No message from Kate since the earlier one that said she'd be seeing the dentist at ten thirty. Mom was taking her.

Holly's confidence took a nose dive. Without Kate, the script had changed. Last night, they'd decided that Holly would talk to Sam Callahan while Kate kept Meredith out of the way. But now that Holly was on her own, Twiggy would have to fill Kate's shoes instead.

Would it work?

Or would Twiggy flub it up?

The waterfall had turned into a slow drizzle by the time they drove into the show grounds. A parking attendant, wearing a neon orange cape that made him look like a traffic cone, directed them to a far corner. Beyond a line of trees, Holly could see blue-and-white striped tents. She cracked open her window and heard an announcement for the NEHC Pleasure Class.

Pleasure?

More like torture in this weather. Holly shivered, glad she wasn't competing.

"Did you girls bring slickers and boots?" Meredith said, as her SUV skidded over ruts the size of small waves.

"Crocs," Twiggy said, holding up a lime green foot. She brandished a matching umbrella. "And this. It's required at all British horse shows. They won't let you in without one."

Expertly, Meredith backed into a parking space between a gooseneck trailer and a camper-van with kids' faces pressed against the windows. Twiggy blew them a kiss.

"Cute," her bodyguard said.

It was almost ten thirty by the time they'd squelched through ankle-deep mud to the entrance gate. Anxiously, Holly checked her phone for a message. Kate would be at the dentist by now.

* * *

Trying not to wince, Kate heard their family dentist diagnose an impacted wisdom tooth. He recommended an oral surgeon. "Doctor Wall is in White River Junction," he said to Liz, "and if you hurry, she can fit you in at eleven fifteen."

Oral surgeon?

Kate blanched and shifted the ice pack to her other

hand. She'd never had a tooth pulled before. Would they jab her with Novocain or knock her out?

Liz told her not to worry. "You won't feel a thing."

White River was a forty-minute drive—close to the New Hampshire border—but it felt like forty hours. Kate's tooth vibrated with pain at every corner and every bump in the road, even though Liz was driving as smoothly and carefully as she always did.

Kate was in agony with the miserable tooth, but even worse was worrying about Holly. By now, she'd be at the show and looking for Sam Callahan. It was hard, keeping all this to herself. For a wild and wooly moment, Kate was tempted to tell Liz. This was pain speaking, not common sense.

Somehow, Kate held it all together.

When they reached the outskirts of White River Junction, Liz turned on her GPS and found the medical building where the dentist was. She supported Kate's elbow as they climbed the stone steps. On either side were faded blue hydrangeas, bent double by the rain. They looked even more miserable than Kate felt.

The dentist's receptionist greeted them with a friendly smile. "Dr. Wall will see you in a minute. Please take a seat."

"Thank you," Liz said. "We really appreciate this."

Yeah, right, Kate thought.

It wasn't Liz about to have a tooth pulled, it was her.

Kate flopped into a chair and felt enormously sorry for herself. The bravado she'd felt that morning had totally vanished, as if it never existed. Shame—or maybe it was guilt—tapped its bony finger on her shoulder.

So what? it said.

Kate tried to ignore it, but it kept tapping until she got up and sat in another chair. It made no difference. This was nothing compared to what Holly had gone through.

The door opened. More patients showed up—a skinny girl wearing shorts and a tank top beneath a clear plastic poncho, followed by a woman twice her size dressed in a voluminous raincoat. They claimed the chairs across from Kate. Immediately, the girl dumped her poncho on the floor and grabbed a copy of *Seventeen*. She had a huge bruise on one shoulder; smaller ones dotted her arms and legs.

"Kate McGregor?" said a voice.

"Here." Liz stood. "Come on," she said to Kate. "Time to face the music."

As Kate stumbled to her feet, another dental assistant arrived. She consulted her clipboard, then looked around the waiting room. "Rebecca DeWitt?" she said.

The skinny girl was too engrossed in her magazine to pay attention until the woman—Kate assumed it was the girl's mother—slapped her bare legs. "Get a move on."

With a scowl, the girl glanced at Kate, then followed the technician. She looked familiar, but why?

Kate shook her head.

She wasn't thinking straight. This dumb tooth had scrambled her brain.

14

DESPITE THE RAIN, classes continued. Kids wearing slickers and helmet covers trotted past on soaking wet ponies. Trainers shouted; parents stood in huddled groups beneath a mountain range of umbrellas. At one point, Holly could've sworn she saw Luke Callahan cantering by on Santiago, his dark bay Thoroughbred.

Well, maybe not.

There were an awful lot of dark bays about. Even the chestnuts and grays looked dark bay in this gloomy weather. The loudspeaker announced another class, but it crackled so badly, Holly could barely hear it.

"What now, boss?" Twiggy said.

Her bodyguard had gone ahead and was out of earshot. At least, Holly hoped she was. "Keep Meredith busy for as long as you can. Ask her to explain stuff about the hunter-jumper circuit. Tell her it's very different from England, and—"

"Yes, ma'am." Twiggy gave a mock salute and stamped her foot like a guard at Buckingham Palace. Water spurted up through the holes in her Crocs. "Where will you be?"

"Trying to find Sam Callahan."

So far, there'd been no sign of him—just a sea of anonymous people looking wet and miserable and probably wishing they were anywhere else but at a horse show.

Holding her green umbrella aloft like Mary Poppins, Twiggy skipped off, sloshing through puddles. Holly waited till she'd caught up with Meredith and they'd gone around the corner toward one of the show rings. Okay, so where was Mr. Callahan? A woman wearing a blue-and-white badge walked past.

A judge?

Holly asked if she knew where Sam Callahan was, but the woman turned out to be a food vendor and she had no idea. "Try the secretary's tent. They'll probably know."

"Where is it?"

The woman pulled a soggy program from her pocket and gave it to Holly. The pages had stuck together. Carefully, she pried them apart and found a map of the show grounds. "Thanks."

It was almost eleven. If she didn't find Sam Callahan before he began judging, she wouldn't have a chance to talk to him until after the show. The thought of staying here all day made her cringe.

Moments later, the drizzle ended and a weak sun began to shine. People shed their raincoats and folded their umbrellas. The loudspeaker announced Green Conformation Hunter in Ring Four.

Sam Callahan's first class.

According to her map, Ring Four was just beyond a group of mobile tack shops and food carts, in the same direction that Twiggy and Meredith had gone. With luck, they wouldn't be hanging about by the rail or browsing the vendors. Holly half ran, half walked toward the ring, and she was almost there when a man with a tweed cap pulled low over his forehead overtook her.

"Mr. Callahan?" she said.

It was a long shot, given she could barely remember what he looked like, but he fit the part—tan breeches tucked into mud-spattered Wellies, the ubiquitous cap, and a dark-blue windbreaker. Pinned to the front was a blue-and-white badge.

He stopped. "Yes?"

Did she have the guts to come right out with it? Did she even have time to explain? The famous trainer was already frowning and looking at his watch. Holly took a deep breath and decided to plunge in.

"You accused Meredith Tudor of doping a horse," she blurted. "Why?"

"And you are—?"

"Holly Chapman," she said, thrusting out her hand. Best to be polite, especially after her rude outburst. Aunt Bea always said you'd catch more flies with honey than with vinegar. "My mother runs Timber Ridge Stables."

"I met her," Sam Callahan said, shaking her hand. His grip was so hard, Holly winced. "At the party for that princess, or whoever she was." He made it sound as if Twiggy were a fake, like the Barbie doll on top of her cake.

From the corner of her eye, Holly could see Twiggy and Meredith, trying on riding helmets beneath a tack vendor's black-and-gold awning. She heard them laugh, then Twiggy stepped back to take a photo of Meredith posing with a mannequin dressed in an old-fashioned side saddle outfit. She wanted to text them.

Stay where you are. Don't come any closer.

"She's a *real* princess, and—" Holly began.

Sam Callahan interrupted. "I have a class to judge and you're wasting my time, so please excuse me." Without another word, he strode off, leaving Holly stranded in the mud and feeling like a complete idiot. She'd really blown it this time.

"Heads up!" someone yelled.

Holly whipped around. *Runaway horse?*

Reins flapping, it galloped toward her—a big bay, showing the whites of its eyes. People scattered like chickens; clumps of mud flew in all directions. With mounting horror, Holly watched as Twiggy aimed her camera at Meredith again. Unaware of the danger, Twiggy took three steps backward, slipped, and landed flat on her back in a very large puddle. If it hadn't been so scary, it would've been funny—the perfect prat fall.

"No!" Holly screamed.

For a split second, she was stuck in slow motion—a cartoon character with its feet nailed to the ground. Her legs had turned to lead, her mind had gone blank. She couldn't move.

But somebody else did.

With a gigantic leap, Meredith Tudor threw herself on top of Twiggy. Nostrils flaring, the horse swerved. He skidded sideways and managed to corkscrew over them, but one of his hooves clipped Meredith's head.

Her body went limp.

As Holly ran toward them, she heard Sam Callahan's voice calling for an ambulance.

"Make it fast," he yelled.

* * *

The medics laid a woozy Meredith on a stretcher, still wearing the helmet she'd been trying on. They placed an oxygen mask over her face and slid her into the ambulance. Off it roared, sirens wailing and lights flashing, even faster than it had arrived.

Twiggy had wanted to go with them. She wasn't hurt; just winded and unspeakably muddy.

"I'll drive you," said Sam Callahan.

After ordering his assistant judge to take over, he ran to his car—parked nearby—and told the girls to get in. At breakneck speed, he followed the ambulance, hurtling down country roads like a race car driver.

"Is she gonna be okay?" Twiggy said. Muddy water dribbled across her shoulders, soaking into the car's luxurious sheepskin seat covers. For a mad moment, Holly wanted to hose her down.

Sam Callahan nodded. "Yes."

"How do you know?" Holly said. She was in the back seat, behind Sam Callahan, gritting her teeth and willing him to go even faster.

"Meredith Tudor is tough."

"But—" Holly began, then caught her breath. This wasn't the right time to start an argument.

Sam Callahan glanced in his rear view mirror. "I'll explain later," he said, overtaking a farm truck on a blind corner. "First, let's get to the hospital and make sure those doctors do their job."

Ten minutes later, they screeched to a halt behind Meredith's empty ambulance. Its rear doors yawned open. Sam Callahan pointed toward the entrance marked Emergency Room and told the girls to go inside. He would park the car and join them.

A large clock on the wall said 11:40.

"Oh, my god," Holly said. "Kate."

She reached for her phone and punched in Kate's number. It went to voice mail. She left a text, then stared at her screen, begging it to respond.

Nothing.

"Are you related to Ms. Tudor?" said the desk clerk when Twiggy demanded to see Meredith. Fingers poised over a keyboard, the woman raised a fierce looking eyebrow. Twiggy gave a noncommittal shrug.

The clerk turned to Holly. "You?"

Holly shook her head. They couldn't get away with lying, not when they were obviously white and Meredith was black. Twiggy tried to bluff her way through.

"I'm her third cousin, four times removed," she told the skeptical desk clerk who was now glaring at the muddy footprints they'd left across the waiting room floor.

"Yeah, right," she said. "And I'm a princess."

That was all Twiggy needed. Before Holly could stop her, she'd whipped out her British passport and stuck it beneath the woman's nose. "I am Princess Isabel of Lunaberg," Twiggy announced in her plummiest voice. "My father, Prince Ferdinand, is tenth in line for the throne."

"Which throne?" said a voice.

Holly cringed, waiting for a raft of really bad jokes about loos and toilets, but none came. "C'mon," she said, steering Twiggy toward the rest room. "You're a mess."

Using half a roll of paper towels, they cleaned themselves up. Twiggy rinsed her muddy hair in the sink, then took off her Crocs and rinsed them as well. Holly wiped the mud off the backs of Twiggy's legs. Moments later, they emerged and headed for a line of gray plastic chairs.

Holly took a seat. She'd spent many hours in hospital waiting rooms, and these chairs were just as uncomfortable as all the others she'd sat in. With agonizing slowness, the clock ticked another minute, then another. Sam Callahan folded his lanky frame into a chair opposite them.

"Any news?" he said.

Twiggy sighed. "They won't tell us what's going on."

"Which reminds me," Holly said, forcing herself to look directly at Luke's father. "You promised to tell me"—she took a deep breath and crossed her fingers—"about Meredith."

* * *

Sam Callahan's explanation came out in bits and snatches, punctuated by urgent voices calling "Stat" and "Code Blue" from a loudspeaker that echoed. Medics charged in with more trauma victims and rushed them through swinging doors marked "No Admittance." Gurneys rattled, lights flashed, and machines bleeped. A man complained that the waiting room's coffeemaker had quit working.

At some point, Luke Callahan arrived with a young woman from the saddlery where Meredith and Twiggy had been trying on helmets. The woman, whose blue-and-white nametag said Cheryl, was in tears.

"Don't cry," Sam Callahan said, handing her a paper napkin. "Your Samshield helmet has probably saved Meredith's life."

Samshield?

Was it named for Sam Callahan?

"No," he said when Holly asked. "I've got nothing to do with it, but I'm mighty glad it was on Meredith's head when that horse ran her over."

"Dad," Luke said, "that was *my* horse."

Everyone looked at him.

"Santiago?" his father said.

Holly knew that Luke had more than one horse. In addition to Santiago, he had two other grand prix jumpers, a youngster he was bringing along, and a Welsh pony called Cupcake he could not bear to get rid of.

Luke nodded. "I'm so sorry."

It looked as if a family explosion was about to happen, so Holly steered the conversation back to Meredith and why Sam Callahan had accused her of doping.

It turned out that he hadn't.

Mrs. Dean had misunderstood him, probably on purpose. She hadn't let Sam Callahan finish telling her about

Meredith—how she'd taken the fall for her trainer. He'd doped her horse, then blamed Meredith when it didn't pass the drug test. The USDF had kicked her out, the trainer got off scot-free, and Meredith's dressage career wound up in tatters.

"Who was her trainer?" Holly said.

Sam Callahan's face turned grim. "Nobody you'd know."

"Try me."

"An English guy," he said. "Vincent—"

"—King?" Holly finished.

In just a few words, she told an astonished Sam Callahan how Liz had thrown Vincent King out of the barn last summer for poling Angela's horse and how he'd turned up in England a couple of months ago, abusing Buccaneer in the show ring.

"Typical," Sam Callahan said, sounding disgusted.

Twiggy glared at him. "Why didn't you help Meredith?"

"It's complicated." A guilty look flashed across the trainer's weathered face.

Holly glanced at Luke, sitting beside his father. Was he also feeling guilty? She didn't blame him for Santiago getting loose. That could happen to anyone. Horses got loose at shows all the time, and sometimes people got hurt.

The ER doors swung open, and a woman in a white coat with a stethoscope around her neck walked up. "I'm

Doctor Greenberg," she said, looking from one to the other. "Are you folks with Meredith Tudor?"

In her hand was the Samshield helmet.

15

For a moment, nobody spoke until Sam Callahan cleared his throat. "Meredith has no family, so you'd best talk to these young ladies," he said, waving toward Holly and Twiggy. "They are her friends."

Twiggy leaped to her feet. "Is she all right?"

"Yes, thanks to this," the doctor said, patting the dented helmet. "Ms. Tudor has a superficial head wound that we stitched up, and a mild concussion. We'll keep her overnight—just for observation—and, barring unforeseen circumstances, she'll be good to go tomorrow morning."

Cheryl held out her hand. "That's our helmet."

"Oh." The doctor gave it to her. "I'm afraid it's ruined."

"I know." A tear ran down Cheryl's pale cheek. "My boss is going to be furious. These helmets are expensive."

"This ought to cover it," Sam Callahan said, pulling out his wallet. He peeled off a wad of bills and handed them to Cheryl. "And tell your boss that I'll be writing an article about helmets for the *Chronicle* and that I will be sure to mention Meredith's accident. I imagine your boss, and Samshield, will appreciate the free publicity."

Cheryl mumbled her thanks and left.

"Can we see Meredith?" Holly said, glaring at Cheryl's retreating back. Her boss didn't deserve a mention in Sam Callahan's article—or anything else for that matter.

Doctor Greenberg nodded. "For just a few minutes."

She led them through the swinging doors into a wide corridor with curtained cubicles on both sides. Meredith managed a weak smile when they entered hers. A bandage circled her head; tubes ran from her left arm to a machine that beeped.

"Are you all right?" she said looking at Twiggy. "You didn't get hurt?"

"Fit as a fiddle," Twiggy declared. "I'm even clean. Well, sort of." She wiped a speck of stray mud off her face, then leaned over and kissed Meredith's cheek. "Thanks for saving me. I guess it makes you a real bodyguard, huh?"

"Yeah, something like that," Meredith said, clearly embarrassed.

A nurse came in and checked the machines that were

monitoring Meredith's blood pressure and heartbeat. "Looking good," she said and left.

Twiggy said, "I can now chalk two things off my American bucket list."

"What?" Holly said.

"Horse shows and hospitals."

Meredith gave a little frown. "How did you kids get here?" she said. "I hope you didn't drive my car."

"No," Twiggy said. "Don't be silly. We got a ride with—"

Holly trod on her foot.

Twiggy glared at her. "Ouch."

"A gate steward dropped us off," Holly said, thinking fast. She eased up on Twiggy's foot and grabbed her arm instead. "We'll be back in a minute," she told Meredith and dragged Twiggy into the corridor.

"What's wrong?" Twiggy said.

"Nothing," Holly whispered. "Just don't tell Meredith about Sam Callahan. She's got enough to worry about."

"Okay," Twiggy said, rubbing her arm. "But I've gotta call my dad. He can't fire Meredith after this."

"I know," Holly said. She'd already thought of that, along with the worry that Prince Ferdinand might decide it was way too dangerous for his daughter to be anywhere near Timber Ridge and he'd order her to come home. Or worse, he'd send Stephan over to collect her.

They had to tread carefully.

But first, they had to defuse Mrs. Dean, and Holly knew exactly how to handle it—as long as Sam Callahan was still in the waiting room.

* * *

She found him at the coffeemaker, trying to make it work. With an exasperated sigh, Sam Callahan held up an empty cup.

"Dad," Luke said, "there's a Starbucks around the corner. What do you want?"

Sitting down, Sam Callahan fired off his order. Luke jangled his car keys and looked at Holly. "What about you?"

"Nothing for me, thanks."

The minute he left, Holly took the chair beside Luke's father, then changed her mind and snagged herself a seat across from him. They needed to be face-to-face.

She said, "You owe Meredith Tudor."

"I know," he said.

All of a sudden, Sam Callahan didn't seem like the BNT that Kate idolized. He was an ordinary human being who'd made a big mistake that needed to be put right. Holly melted a little. "I have an idea," she said.

He looked at her. "What?"

"First, you will call Mrs. Dean and make sure she understands that Meredith is not guilty of doping a horse. And second, I want you to phone Prince Ferdinand and tell him to call off the dogs."

"Prince Ferdi—?"

"Twiggy's father," Holly said, as Sam Callahan's eyes grew wide. She wrote down both phone numbers on a napkin and gave them to him. "And, yes, she really *is* a princess."

* * *

By the time Twiggy returned from Meredith's cubicle, Holly felt as if she'd actually accomplished something. In addition to convincing Prince Ferdinand not to fire Meredith, Sam Callahan had also convinced him to pay Meredith's hospital bill if her insurance didn't cover it. But he hadn't been able to reach Mrs. Dean.

"I'll tell her in person," he said, offering to drive Holly and Twiggy back to Timber Ridge. While there, he would confront Mrs. Dean.

"What about Meredith's car?" Holly said.

Sam Callahan stood up. "Luke and I will take care of it," he said. "We'll also bring Meredith home tomorrow, assuming they let her go."

"*If* she agrees to go with you," Holly said. "You're not exactly her favorite person." This was a guess, based on what Kate had told her, but from the look on Mr. Callahan's face, it had struck a nerve.

He said, "I aim to put that right. By the time I get through with the USDF, they'll be begging to have her back."

"But she doesn't have a horse," Twiggy said.

Sam Callahan took a sip of coffee from the enormous cup Luke had just given him. "I have plenty. In fact, I've got a hot dressage prospect that needs a strong rider. Meredith Tudor will be perfect."

Holly began to feel warm and fuzzy inside. This had worked out way better than she'd ever dreamed it would. As she followed Twiggy and the Callahans into the parking lot, her cell phone pinged. A text from Kate with a bunch of frowny faces—

Tooth out. Am groggy. Talk later.

Bummer, Holly texted back, then didn't know what else to say. Clearly, Kate was in no shape to hear about Sam Callahan and Meredith's miraculous save. When they reached his father's car, Luke gave Holly a high five.

"Tell Kate 'hi' from me," he said.

"Okay."

With a lopsided grin, Luke hopped into his truck. Rolling down his window, he leaned out looking so gorgeous that Holly wanted to melt. "Don't forget."

"I won't," she said, feeling even warmer and fuzzier. In fact, she even felt herself blush. No, wait a minute. That was Kate's job.

If only she hadn't missed all this.

* * *

As they approached Timber Ridge, Twiggy said she didn't want to spend the night at the Dean's house without Meredith.

"Can I bunk in with you guys?"

"You bet," Holly said.

"Cool," Twiggy said, then pulled a pouty face. "But I don't have a toothbrush."

"You can borrow mine."

"Yuck."

"We'll have a pajama party," Holly said, hoping that Kate would be up for it.

Then there was Mom.

Would she have a meltdown because Holly had disobeyed orders, never mind that everything had worked out? She decided to text Mom a heads-up.

Home soon. Don't panic, but Meredith in hospital. Doc says she will be fine.

Sam Callahan dropped them at the top of Holly's driveway and said he'd be in touch. Holly was tempted to wish him luck with Mrs. Dean.

Instead, she crossed her fingers.

With adults you never knew if they'd fink out or really follow through with exactly what they promised.

* * *

From far away, Kate heard noises—muffled and indistinct. Dishes rattled; cupboards opened and closed. Something—a spoon, probably—clattered onto the kitchen floor. Then silence—sweet silence—but only for a second or two. Twiggy's squeal resonated loud and clear.

"Ice cream?"

"In the freezer," came Holly's voice.

Kate pulled a pillow over her head and tried to block them out. Moments later, her bedroom door cracked open.

"Are you awake?" Holly said.

Kate sat up, feeling dizzy. "I am now."

Her sister tiptoed into the room, followed by Twiggy. They sat on Holly's bed, looking at Kate. They probably had concern written all over their faces, but it was hard to see. Kate tugged at the window shade above her bed, and all of a sudden the room was flooded with light.

She blinked. "What time is it?"

"Four o'clock," Holly said. "How's your tooth?"

"S'okay," Kate mumbled.

It wasn't really. It hurt a lot more than she'd thought it would, but the oral surgeon said that was to be expected. It would take a few days for the empty socket to heal. Holly offered Kate a dish brimming with chocolate chip ice cream.

"Want some?"

"No, thanks." The very idea of food—even ice cream—made her queasy. The doc had warned her about that, too. Kate hugged her pillow.

"I talked to Sam Callahan," Holly said.

"And?"

"Meredith's in the clear."

"Tell me," Kate said, loving every minute of Holly's explanation. This was so cool. Beyond cool. It was all that they'd hoped for, and a whole lot more. Despite her stupid tooth, Kate wanted to dance around the room and punch the air with her fist, but her sluggish head wouldn't cooperate.

"So," Holly said. "What happened at the dentist?"

"No big deal," Kate said, aiming for a nonchalance she didn't quite feel. "I got a wisdom tooth pulled, and—"

"Yikes," Twiggy said. "That must've been awful. Weren't you scared?"

"Yes, but—"

Images of that girl swam into Kate's view—the bruises on her arms and the way she'd stared at Kate as if they knew one another. This was a whole lot more scary than her dumb wisdom tooth. Sucking in her breath, Kate willed herself to remember. But all she came up with was a blank.

"What's wrong?" Holly said. "Are you okay?"

Kate nodded. "Yeah, I'm fine," she said, but the girl's name kept hovering, just out of reach, Taunting her. It began with R. Was it Rachel or Rita or—?

"Rebecca?" Kate said. "Does it mean anything to you."

"No," Holly said. "Should it?"

"That girl who's been following you," Kate said, still grasping at straws. "I think I saw her at the dentist."

"What girl?" Twiggy scooped up the last of her ice cream, then licked the bowl. "Yummy."

Holly shrugged. "Kate's convinced I've got a stalker."

"Join the club," Twiggy said with an elaborate sigh. "I've had hundreds. It's why I've got a bodyguard."

"What's her last name?" Holly said.

"Tudor," answered Twiggy.

"Not Meredith, you idiot," Holly said. "The girl Kate saw."

Kate dug even deeper. Why was her head so fuzzy? She ran the scenario again—Liz leading her out of the waiting room, the dental assistant who'd interrupted them by asking for—

"Rebecca DeWitt?" Kate said.

Holly gasped. "Becca?"

Becca . . . Rebecca . . . the name rang so many bells that Kate couldn't believe she'd missed the connection. This was the girl who'd come to Holly's pool party last year, a month before Kate had arrived at Timber Ridge. “Isn’t she the girl Angela said was too fat to wear a bikini?”

16

MISERABLY, HOLLY NODDED. She'd shoved Angela into the pool for that one. The water had made a satisfying mess of Angela's mascara and expensive new hairdo, but it hadn't stopped her from taunting poor Becca.

"Well, she isn't fat now," Kate said. "She's skinny as a rail."

Kate had to be mistaken. This girl—the stalker—couldn't possibly be the overweight girl Holly had met on Facebook and been BFFs with for almost a year. That girl had dark brown hair, not blond, and her nails had been bitten to the quick.

"Did Mom see her?" Holly said. "In the waiting room?"

"I guess so."

"But she didn't recognize her?"

Kate shrugged. "I don't know. I was kind of busy, trying not to die."

"Didn't you take a photo of her?" Twiggy said, whipping out her cell phone and aiming it at Kate. "Like, you know, for evidence?"

"This isn't Nancy Drew," Holly said.

The princess snapped off a picture of Holly's old wooden rocking horse. It had almost broken when Becca had sat on it. "I didn't have have Nancy Drew books in England," Twiggy complained, as if she'd been cheated.

"No, really," Kate said. "It's a good idea. You must have a picture of her, Holly. It was your half-birthday party, remember?"

"I think I deleted them all."

"Go and look, anyway."

"Anyone for more ice cream?" Twiggy said.

"Can't," Kate said, cupping her jaw. "Maybe later."

"Okay, sure," Twiggy said and skipped off.

Holly booted up her laptop, and with only a few clicks, she found the right folder. Inside were dozens of photos of last year's half-birthday party. She scrolled through them all. There was Angela in a pink bikini, her best friend Denise in yellow, Robin and Sue goofing about on the diving board . . . and there was Becca in her baggy shorts with a smudge of chocolate on her double chin, about to eat another slice of cake.

Poor, sad Becca.

Holly hated what had happened, but it wasn't her fault. Becca couldn't deal with the fact that Holly was in a wheelchair. They'd been planning a sleepover after the party, but Becca had told her mother to take her home.

They lived in New Hampshire.

Her town was just over the state line from White River Junction where Kate had gotten her wisdom tooth pulled out. Holly enlarged Becca's photo and showed it to Kate, hoping against hope it was a different girl. But it wasn't.

"That's her," Kate said.

"Are you sure?"

"She's lost weight, dyed her hair blond, and grown her nails," Kate said, which shocked Holly to the core because Kate didn't normally pay attention to details like this. "But, yes, it's the same girl."

With a sigh, Holly closed Becca's picture.

Kate said, "What are you going to do?"

Holly thought long and hard. Becca wasn't malicious; she was in a world of hurt. Witness the bruises that Kate had described. Becca's mother was probably beating her up, or somebody else was. This was why she was lashing out. She'd wanted to hurt someone, and Holly had been an easy target.

"I'm gonna tell Mom," Holly finally said, wondering where Twiggy had gone. It didn't take *that* long to serve herself another dish of ice cream. "She'll know what to do, and if she doesn't, she'll know where to get help."

"For Becca?"

"Yes."

Kate sighed. "Good call."

Something made a noise beyond their window. Holly leaned across Kate's bed and raised the screen. Tapestry's velvety nose poked inside.

"She wants to give Kate a kiss," Twiggy said.

"Why?"

"To make her feel better."

While Kate slathered her mare with kisses, Holly remembered Luke Callahan's message.

Tell Kate I said 'hi.'

Kate was going to love this, but it would make more of an impact tomorrow, after her tooth had calmed down and Meredith was back here, where she belonged.

Book 13, HIGH STAKES

No matter how hard she tries, Princess Twiggy cannot stay out of trouble. Her father has laid down strict rules, and Twiggy manages to break all of them. Flying beneath the royal radar, the headstrong princess drags her best friends into yet another harebrained adventure.

Except this one turns dangerous.

It also drives a wedge between Kate and Holly, who are trying to get ready for an important horse show that Mrs. Dean is pushing for. Angela runs hot and cold on this, which ramps up Kate's suspicions.

Holly is concerned, too.

But their worries about Angela's erratic behavior take a back seat when they're confronted with a rival team that's bent on destroying Timber Ridge.

Sign up for our mailing list and be among the first to know when the next Timber Ridge Riders book will be out. Send your email address to:

timberridgeriders@gmail.com

For more information about the series, visit:
www.timberridgeriders.com

or check out our Facebook page:
www.facebook.com/TimberRidgeRiders

Note: all email addresses are kept strictly confidential.

About the Author

MAGGIE DANA'S FIRST RIDING LESSON, at the age of five, was less than wonderful. She hated it so much, she didn't try again for another three years. But all it took was the right horse and the right instructor and she was hooked.

After that, Maggie begged for her own pony and was lucky enough to get one. Smoky was a black New Forest pony who loved to eat vanilla pudding and drink tea, and he became her constant companion. Maggie even rode him to school one day and tethered him to the bicycle rack . . . but not for long because all the other kids wanted pony rides, much to their teachers' dismay.

Maggie and Smoky competed in Pony Club trials and won several ribbons. But mostly, they had fun—trail riding and hanging out with other horse-crazy girls. At horse camp, Maggie and her teammates spent one night sleeping in the barn, except they didn't get much sleep because the horses snored. The next morning, everyone was tired and cranky, especially when told to jump without stirrups.

Born and raised in England, Maggie now makes her home on the Connecticut shoreline. When not mucking stalls or grooming shaggy ponies, Maggie enjoys spending time with her family and writing the next book in her TIMBER RIDGE RIDERS series.

Printed in Great Britain
by Amazon